"Can I get you something?" Watching her disrobe, I felt an odd lump in my throat.

"You can get your ass over here, slide into this bed and hold me," she said. "I can't seem to stop shaking." She pulled back the covers and slid underneath them, curling into a fetal position.

"Uh, maybe I should get you a blanket . . ."

"Honest, Cass. I just need to be held."

Dutifully, but with an accelerated pulse, I stripped down to my underwear and shirt and did as she asked.

I inched up against her and wrapped my arm around her waist, careful not to let my hand slide any higher or lower as I pulled her against me. We were touching the entire length of our bodies, and I buried my face in her hair, breathing in the scent I knew so well.

LOOKING FOR NAIAD?

Buy our books at
www.naiadpress.com

or call our toll-free number
1-800-533-1973

or by fax (24 hours a day)
1-850-539-9731

6TH Sense

A CASSIDY JAMES MYSTERY

KATE CALLOWAY

THE NAIAD PRESS, INC.
1999

Printed in the United States of America on acid-free paper
First Edition

Editor: Christine Cassidy
Cover designer: Bonnie Liss (Phoenix Graphics)
Typesetter: Sandi Stancil

Library of Congress Cataloging-in-Publication Data

Calloway, Kate, 1957 –
  Sixth sense : a Cassidy James mystery / by Kate Calloway.
     p.   cm.
  ISBN 1-56280-228-3   (alk. paper)
  I. Title.
PS3553.A4245S5   1999
813'.54—dc21
                                                    98-44746
                                                        CIP

For my mom and sister,
with whom I've shared
many wonderful psychic moments.

Acknowledgments

A heartfelt thanks to my friends (again!) for taking the time to read and critique a work in progress: Murrell, Linda, Carolyn, Deva, and especially Carol who keeps me honest! Thanks, too, to Christi Cassidy for her enthusiastic encouragement and unerring eye, and to all my friends and family for their continued support. Finally, thanks to those readers who have offered such kind feedback and support in their letters, reviews and notes on the Internet. You make these books all the more fun to write!

About the Author

Kate Calloway was born in 1957. She has published several novels with Naiad including *First Impressions, Second Fiddle, Third Degree, Fourth Down* and *Fifth Wheel,* all in the Cassidy James Mystery Series. Her short stories appear in the Naiad anthologies *Lady Be Good* and *Dancing in the Dark.* Her hobbies include cooking, winetasting, boating, songwriting and spending time with Carol. They split their time between southern California and the Pacific Northwest, setting for the Cassidy James novels. Those who know Kate well say that Cassidy James is not entirely fictional.

Chapter One

"Don't hang up," she said.

"Maggie?" My voice cracked in disbelief more than uncertainty.

"I know you don't want to see me, Cass. And I have no right to ask this of you. But I need help."

"Go on." My heart was hammering.

"I think I saw someone being murdered."

I paused, letting the words sink in. "Let me give you Martha's number," I said finally. Martha was my best friend and a detective on the Kings Harbor Police Force.

"I still know her number, Cass. It's you I need right now. Will you at least hear me out? I wouldn't ask if this weren't important." Before I could respond, she went on. "I'm at the county dock. If you don't want to come pick me up, I can rent a boat."

"No," I said too hastily. "I'll meet you at Lizzie's."

There was no way I wanted Maggie Carradine in my house. Lizzie's would be full of noisy locals which would provide a much safer environment for my first encounter with Maggie since her return to Oregon.

"Thank you," she whispered. The line went dead and I was left holding the receiver against my cheek.

I grabbed my boat keys, called good-bye to the cats and jogged down the rampway to my boat.

Spring had finally arrived in Cedar Hills, and the late afternoon sunshine was bouncing off Rainbow Lake in a vain attempt to warm the nippy air. A westerly breeze rippled the water as I sped toward town in my blue, open-bow Sea Swirl. The canvas top was up but even so, I hugged my jacket around me. It wasn't the cool air that had me chilled, though. It was the prospect of seeing Maggie Carradine.

When she had first left for Paris to take care of an ex-lover who was dying, I could scarcely believe it. Out of the blue, she had announced her decision, and there wasn't a thing I could say or do about it. It was a noble mission, an act of kindness, and I did my best to be supportive, but in truth, I was hurt. When the ex had gone into remission and they'd decided to traipse off to Switzerland together, my hurt slid right into anger.

2

I'm not normally the moody, disconsolate type, and mooning around didn't suit me. After many long nights of self-analysis, I finally gave myself permission to get on with my life, and I even began dating another woman. Though brief, my time with Lauren had been passionate and made me feel alive again. Now, months later, just when I was feeling like my old, confident self again, here came Maggie asking for help. I'd known she was back in town, of course, but, so far, had managed to avoid her. I steeled myself against the unexpected fluttering in my stomach and tried to concentrate on the fact that someone had been killed.

Lizzie's is really named Loggers Tavern, but nobody calls it that. Located across from McGregors, the only grocery store in Cedar Hills, it's the favorite watering hole for most locals. By the time I docked at the marina and made my way to Main Street, it was nearly five and the tavern was bustling with the usual Friday evening crowd. Lizzie Thompson greeted me from behind the bar as I squinted in the dimly lit room.

"She's in the back!" she called. I waved my thanks and headed for the far corner.

Maggie sat against the wall, her dark curls framing high cheekbones and green eyes that never failed to unnerve me. She had lost weight, I noticed. Not that she had needed to. She looked almost gaunt and her eyes had a haunted look I hadn't seen before. There was sadness there. And maybe fear. But the change did nothing to make her less striking.

"Thanks for coming." She pushed a glass of Cabernet toward me as I slid into the seat across from her. She had taken the liberty of ordering for me and

I wasn't sure how I felt about it. "You look good," she said. Her gaze was intense as she studied me, making me instantly uncomfortable.

"You've lost weight," I pointed out.

She nodded, sipping her wine.

"I was sorry to hear about Cecily. I mean, I can imagine how difficult that must have been." She shrugged. "What's this about a murder?" I finally asked.

She swallowed and met my gaze. "I'm not sure how to say this so you don't think I'm nuts."

"Don't worry about what I think. Just tell me."

Maggie looked at me, her green eyes pleading with me to understand. "I dreamed someone was killed and then they were."

Anyone else, I would've thanked her for the wine and gotten the hell out of there. But this was Maggie Carradine. She wasn't prone to exaggeration. She didn't make things up. She wasn't overly dramatic. She was a trained psychologist with both feet on the ground, a clear, sharp mind and a big heart. Unless she'd gone completely around the bend, I thought, taking a sip of my wine.

"I know what you're thinking, Cass. Just hear me out. You probably know that when I came back I pretty much had to start my practice from scratch."

I nodded. I knew it hadn't been easy. She'd not only left me when she went to Paris, but she'd left her entire clientele, farming them out to colleagues in Kings Harbor and neighboring towns. Now that she had returned, she couldn't just take them back. I'd heard she was working in other towns, as far away as Eugene, although her office was still in Kings Harbor, just ten miles away from my place.

4

"About six weeks ago," she went on, "I started a therapy group. Victims of Abuse. I've had the idea for some time, and when I ran it by my colleagues, they referred some of their clients to me. It's really taken off. I've got people coming from all over. We meet twice a week."

"You meet in Kings Harbor?"

"Yes. It's actually the most central location. And I can use my own office. Anyway, last Wednesday, I had a dream in which I was killing someone, hitting them over and over with a baseball bat. It was horribly gruesome and I woke up quite disturbed. I didn't know who I'd been killing or why. And I wasn't really myself in the dream. It was more like I'd stepped into someone else's body. You know how that happens sometimes in dreams, where you're someone else?"

I nodded and Maggie drew a deep breath.

"It never dawned on me that it might be a premonition, Cass. I know you've always teased me about being psychic, but this is different. I've never thought I was anywhere close to being clairvoyant. But what happened the next day really blew my mind." She sipped her wine, her green eyes holding mine. "You know how I feel about client confidentiality. But I realize that if I want your help, I'm going to have to tell you things I normally wouldn't."

"Go on," I said.

"One of the group members is a nineteen-year-old, a real sweetheart named Stella Cane. She revealed to the group about a week ago that she'd been beaten by her boyfriend, Hector Peña, since she was fourteen. She loved him, she said. He was good to her most of the time, but he was possessive, overly jealous, and had a temper. She wanted to marry him more than

5

anything in the world. She already had one child by him, but she was afraid of him. And now he'd hit the baby, a three-year-old. Naturally, the other group members were adamant. She should lose the bum, take the kid and run. It's funny how they give advice so easily to one another . . . Anyway, on Thursday, the night after my dream, Stella came in hysterical. Hector was dead. He'd been beaten to death. Bludgeoned with a baseball bat."

"Good God."

"Exactly. I don't think I heard a thing anyone said the rest of that session. I have no idea what I said. My heart was absolutely racing."

"Are you saying you somehow witnessed this guy's murder while you were dreaming? Is that what you think?"

Maggie sighed. "I don't know."

"Is it possible that somehow this Stella telegraphed her intentions to you while you were sleeping? I mean, could she have killed him and for some reason you picked up on what she was doing?"

Maggie shook her head and shrugged. "I just don't know. I'm sure the police consider her a suspect, though. She's from Eugene, and when she didn't make it to this Tuesday's session, I called several times. There was no answer at the number she gave me. I think it was the boyfriend's apartment." She paused, playing with the ring on her finger. It was one I had given her. Not a wedding band or engagement ring. Just a silver and turquoise band that she'd admired at a county fair. That she still wore it surprised me. "You want to hear the weird part?"

"We haven't gotten to the weird part?"

6

Maggie managed a weak smile. "*Weird* might not be the right word. Last night, I had another dream. This time I killed an old man. It was totally different from the first dream. Not as violent, but just as upsetting. The man was old and frail but still able to get around in his electric wheelchair. He drove it right to the edge of a cliff, overlooking the ocean. He was enjoying the breeze, watching a fishing boat on the horizon. I sneaked up behind him, released the brake and gave his chair a fierce push. I leaned over the edge of the cliff and watched his body smash against the rocks. The whole time he was falling, I was laughing."

"Maggie, maybe you should talk to someone about these dreams. I mean one of your colleagues."

Her laugh was short and painful. "Yes. I've thought of that. But I don't think I'm losing it, Cass. I think I'm seeing something that's actually happening. This morning I found this in the *Herald*." She unfolded a newspaper and pushed it across the table. It was on an inside page under "Happenings Up and Down the Coast," a weekly column with local news and tidbits. It was just a paragraph. Still, I read it over several times.

Maynard Ferguson, 84, fell to his death yesterday on the cliffs near his oceanfront estate in Gold Beach. An autopsy is pending. The police hope to learn whether the octogenarian, who had a history of heart problems, suffered an attack prior to the fall. The son of famed lumber baron Pike Ferguson, Maynard is survived by his son, Jake, also of Gold Beach, and a granddaughter, Maylene MacIntyre, who currently resides in Bandon.

"You're right, *weird* isn't quite strong enough."

"Maylene MacIntyre is one of the members in my group."

Her words sent chills down my spine. "I'm afraid to ask, but what is Maylene's history?" I felt like I knew the answer before I asked.

"Sexually molested by her grandfather most of her childhood. Her family never knew and she never told. In fact, she claims she didn't even remember until recently. A classic case of repressed memory. She's almost forty and just now dealing with the trauma of all this. She said that before he died, she wanted to confront him about it, let him know that he'd ruined her life. Both of her short marriages were a disaster and she hasn't been able to have a normal sexual relationship with anyone her whole life."

I drained my wine glass and looked around for Lizzie. She must've been watching because before I could turn my head, she was setting two fresh glasses on the table.

"She looks good, doesn't she?" she said, pointing her chin at Maggie.

I nodded politely. No way was I going to get into a discussion about how good Maggie looked. "Why haven't you called the police?" I asked when Lizzie was out of earshot.

"And tell them what? That I think I'm dreaming murders before they happen? I can see the look on their faces now. Besides, no one said the old man was actually murdered."

"Martha would listen, Maggie."

"Martha has no jurisdiction. The first one happened in Eugene, the last one in Gold Beach. The only connection between them is that both victims were connected to clients of mine."

"Jesus, Maggie. They weren't just connected! They were the people victimizing your clients. Someone is killing the people who have abused your clients. It could be someone in the group itself."

"Maybe. I mean, it's possible the old man did kill himself." I arched an eyebrow and she sighed. "Just because for some unexplainable reason I'm picking up on these deaths doesn't mean that someone in the group is killing them. I mean, maybe I've just tuned into these guys because I've been hearing about them. They may be totally unrelated." We stared at each other in gloomy silence. "Okay," she finally said, sipping her wine. "Let's say that what you're thinking and what I'm thinking is right, that someone in the group killed those two people. Why am I dreaming it? And what in the hell am I going to do about it? "

"I don't know, Mag. You're the expert on psychology. Isn't there something in those books you study that deals with this?"

She laughed. "Having prior knowledge of a murder isn't exactly standard textbook psychology. It's more in the realm of parapsychology, which isn't my area of expertise. I've been racking my brain, trying to think of someone who might help me understand what's happening. I have no idea why I'd suddenly start experiencing this kind of premonition. It doesn't make sense." I started to speak but she cut me off. "And don't tell me I've always been psychic because this is totally different. I'm scared to death."

"I know you are, Maggie. That's why I think you should call Martha."

"And have the police question every group member? I'm bound by client-confidentiality. It's bad enough I'm telling you. It's not that I don't trust Martha, but then she'd have to tell someone else, and the whole thing would be out of my control."

"It's already out of your control, Mag. What if someone else is killed? Are you willing to take that chance?"

"Are you willing to help me?"

The ball was in my court. I could get up and walk out now and she'd have no choice but to call the police. Which is what she should have done in the first place. But would she? I sipped my wine, mentally going over my schedule. I'd just finished working on a runaway teen case, which had ended when the kid, finally out of cash, had decided to come back home. I knew full well that my schedule was clear. So what was stopping me? It's not like I needed the money, I thought. When my first lover, Diane, passed away, I'd suddenly found myself the beneficiary of her sizable estate and life insurance policy. Not knowing what else to do, I numbly agreed to let a stock broker friend of mine invest the money for me. I hadn't paid much attention at first, but when, in less than a year, the money had nearly doubled, I began to take notice. As my friend wheeled and dealed on my behalf, the market continued to boom and my investments grew by leaps and bounds.

So I quit my job as a teacher, moved to Oregon, bought a lake-front house and thought about what I wanted to do with the rest of my life. I hadn't become a private investigator for the money. I'd done it because I had some weird impulse to right the world's wrongs, to thwart the bad guys. I wanted my life to count for something. I wanted to make a difference. I sighed and looked at Maggie. "What do you want me to do?"

"I want you to join the group."

Slowly, I nodded, knowing this was a good idea, even if it *was* the last thing in the world I wanted to do. Maggie must have read my hesitation.

"I need someone who's objective to see what's happening, Cass. I need to know if this whole thing is some unexplainable coincidence, or if one or more of the group members really is out there killing people. Before I go to the police with this, I've got to have a better idea of what's happening."

I leaned back in the chair and studied the ceiling. My head was reeling and it wasn't the wine. I did not want to do this. I certainly did not want to join some therapy group mediated by Maggie Carradine. The idea of sitting in a closed room across from her, talking about inner secrets, seemed unbearable. I wasn't even comfortable being this close to her now.

"You've always been so easy to read," she said, smiling. A blush rode right up my face.

"Yeah, well. That's because you've always been psychic."

"Not with everyone, you know. You were always so open. And you used to know what I was thinking, too. Remember?"

Of course I remembered. I remembered everything about our time together. "Look, Maggie, I don't think this is such a hot idea."

"Cass, I'm not asking you to forgive me. I'm not asking you to be cordial, even. This isn't a date. I want to hire you to find out if one of my clients is a murderer. If I knew another way to do this, I'd try that first. You think this is easy for me, coming here when I know how much you must despise me?" There were tears in her eyes and I felt my throat clamp up.

"I don't hate you, Maggie." It was all I could get out.

"It was a stupid idea," she said, getting to her feet.

"Well, you know me," I said, pushing back my chair. "A sucker for stupid ideas if ever there was one."

We were both standing now, inches apart. Her green eyes still brimmed with emotion. "You'll do it?"

I took a deep breath. "Yes," I said.

And cursed myself the entire way back across Rainbow Lake.

Chapter Two

Whenever I'm upset, I cook. As soon as I got home, I put *Phantom of the Opera* on the CD player and set about making a loaf of sourdough. There is something relaxing about kneading dough. The rhythmic push and pull began to calm me as my fingers coaxed the mound into a silky texture. Finally, I set the loaf in a bowl to rise and looked around at the floury mess, deciding I might as well make some pasta while I was at it. Since the moment I'd heard Maggie's voice on the phone, my insides had been in turmoil. But by the time I had strands of linguini draped over the dowels spread around the kitchen, I was beginning to think more clearly.

While the pasta dried, I punched down the bread and put it in the oven, then chopped red bell peppers, onions, mushrooms and garlic to saute in the olive oil that was heating on the stove. When the vegetables were done, I poured some wine into the pan and poured myself a small glass. With nothing left to do but boil the pasta, I turned off the music and tried to concentrate on what I'd gotten myself into.

It was true that Maggie had always been a little psychic. In fact, the two of us had often been on the same wavelength. I'd been that way with my first lover, Diane. I was that way to some extent with Martha. But Maggie and I had shared an almost eerie ability to tune into each other's feelings.

Not that either one of us could control it, I thought, remembering a time we'd tried just that. We'd both come to the conclusion that whatever extra-sensory powers we possessed were somehow beyond our control. A thought would emerge, unbidden, like a snatch of a song, and we'd both blurt it out at the same time. Images would pop into my head nano-seconds before Maggie would describe exactly what I was seeing. She said the same happened to her and I believed her.

Whether influenced by the moon, the time of month, or some other hidden force, we began to notice a definite pattern in our psychic cycles. Whereas we might go three weeks without a particularly noticeable psychic experience, in the span of a few days we'd have literally dozens. It became natural for us to spend a lot of time together during those days. It was also the time we had the most extraordinary sex.

14

I did not want to think about that, though. I closed my eyes against the image, willing myself to concentrate on the facts. Even accepting the idea that Maggie was more psychic than your average person, why would she suddenly become clairvoyant? Was that possible? And was that really what was happening? The truth was, I didn't know all that much about extrasensory perception beyond my own experiences. If I was going to understand what was happening to Maggie, I'd need to learn more about ESP in general.

I was almost through with dinner when I decided what to do. While my laptop booted up, I cleared the dishes, gave both cats a kitty treat and then bit the bullet and called Maggie. When she didn't answer her home phone, I tried the office number.

"Dr. Carradine's office, can I help you?"

The voice threw me. Young with a slightly Southern lilt. Maggie must have hired a secretary. But wasn't it kind of late for her to be working?

"Hi. Is Maggie in?"

"Uh, just a sec. She's upstairs, I think." The woman sounded young and perky, and a ridiculous stab of jealousy knifed through me. A minute later, Maggie's voice came on the line.

"Who's the teenybopper?" I asked. I couldn't help it.

Maggie chuckled. "That's Buddy, my new assistant. She's just a college kid, but she's a godsend. I'm finally computerizing all my files. What's up? You haven't changed your mind?"

I didn't tell her how tempting that sounded. "Just doing a little preliminary homework. What I need are the names and addresses of the group members."

"Cass, you can't question them. They have to

think you're a client, part of the group. If they see you beforehand, it won't work."

"Give me a little credit here. No one's going to see me. I just want to know a bit about these people before we actually meet."

She sighed. "I'm sorry. That was stupid of me. Hang on, I'll get my files."

After I copied the pertinent information, I told her my plan to search the Internet for sites that might help explain what Maggie was experiencing.

"You're going to join a chat group?"

"Well, it's worth a try. And I'm also going to talk to Martha. I know you don't want the police involved, but you've got to trust me on this one too. I won't give her all the names or specifics, so you don't have to worry about confidentiality. I just want to get her perspective . . ." Before I could go on, Maggie's phone started beeping.

"Damn," she said over the noise.

"What's wrong?"

"Oh, nothing. It's this new phone system. Buddy hasn't quite got the hang of it yet. She must be trying to transfer another call. I've been trying to reach Stella Cane all evening. It could be her." I let her go, thinking that I'd like to talk to Stella Cane myself.

Instead, I folded myself onto the floor and sat in front my coffee table. I knew it would be more ergonomically correct to go into my study, but I preferred to stay with the cats near the warmth of the fireplace. While Panic swatted a half-chewed toy mouse around the living room and Gammon rolled onto her back so that I could rub her impressive belly, I began scanning chat groups. I was amazed at the range of topics. I was tempted to join a few, just for laughs. Raunchy

Poets, Beer Lovers, Cowgirls Looking for Studs on Steeds, Believers in Hale-Bopp's Second Coming — the list was endless. I selected a search engine and typed in Psychics. A new list appeared, almost as intriguing as the first. There were subjects ranging from Near-Death Experiences to Angel Experiences, Psychokinesis to Telekinesis, Out-of-Body Experiences to Friends of Aliens. There were regional groups, age-oriented groups, you name it. I finally opted for PSI-Chat NorthWest and registered to join.

There were currently seven people registered but no one was actually chatting. I decided the fastest way to get what I wanted was to leave a message on their bulletin board and hope that someone would get back to me.

"Help!" I wrote. "Novice psychic needs to know more. Especially interested in dreams that seem clairvoyant. Can you enlighten me? Is it possible to dream something that happens to someone else before it actually happens? Call me Just Curious."

After a brief hesitation, I left my e-mail address and waited. I don't know what I expected, but I was disappointed when, an hour later, I still hadn't received a reply. Apparently all the psychics were sleeping. I decided to join them and hauled myself off to bed, the cats following faithfully behind me.

Chapter Three

Panic had taken to attacking anything that moved beneath the blankets, so when I inadvertently scratched a thigh the next morning, she pounced. Gammon, her portly, much better-mannered sister, let out a huge yawn. Panic had landed close enough to my bladder to propel me out of bed. This, of course, led them both to believe it was time to go outside.

Going outside was the highlight of every morning, rain or shine. There were moles to catch, robins to chase, and untold numbers of mysteries to sniff. I opened the sliding glass door a crack and got the coffeepot going.

Living on the lake had become second nature to me. I no longer thought of it as an adventure, though it often was. I loved the rugged landscape surrounding me. I had a creek running right under my house and a forest surrounding me on three sides. The only way I could get to any of it was by boat across Rainbow Lake.

The lake itself was a huge tangle of waterways that meandered for miles along the tree-covered shoreline. My human neighbors were few and far between, just the way I liked it. There was no shortage, however, of deer, bear and other four-legged creatures, and I'd learned to respect them even as they had learned to tolerate me.

I took my coffee out on the deck, enjoying the crisp morning air, and watched Panic stalk a robin. It was late April, and the hydrangea bushes along the creek were loaded with blue buds, almost ready to explode in their annual gaudy display of color. Gammon was already sprawled on a deck chair, sunning her huge belly.

"You think I'm being foolish?" I asked Gammon. She had large, intelligent eyes the color of gooseberries and she regarded me serenely. "Of course you do. But what am I supposed to do? Let her go through this alone? She could be in danger."

Gammon blinked and began washing her nether regions. Sighing, I went inside to call Martha Harper.

"Girlfriend! I was just thinking about you."

"Don't get started on that psychic stuff, Martha."

"What?"

I explained about Maggie's dreams and the subsequent deaths, skipping over as many details as I could. When I told her I was going to join the therapy group, Martha cut me off.

"You're saying Maggie's seeing these murders before they happen? Are you sure?"

"Of course I'm not sure. But she is. She's really freaked, Martha, and she can't go to the police. She's afraid they'll want to talk to her clients, which of course they would. That would jeopardize her client confidentiality. So I guess I'm it."

"That's dicey, Cass. She could be withholding evidence."

"Since when is a dream evidence?"

She sighed. "You've got a point." We let the silence stretch between us. "Still," she finally said, "I don't know. How do you feel about it?"

"About the psychic part?"

"About the Maggie part. Working with her."

"Oh, that."

"Oh, boy."

"What's that supposed to mean?"

"You know damn well what that means. You're weakening already."

"No way. Absolutely no way, Martha. I've been burned once by her. I'm not about to let it happen again. This is strictly business. Really."

"Okay. I'm glad to hear it. I don't think I could stand to see you hurt again, that's all. I think she blew it big-time and I told her so last time I saw her."

"You saw her? When was this? Why didn't you tell me?"

"It was no big deal, Cass. We just ran into each

other. She looked pretty good, I thought. She's lost weight."

"Yeah, well. I hadn't noticed."

"Uh-huh. Anyway, I made it real clear to her that you didn't need any more grief on her account. Of course, she was typical Maggie. You know — understanding, full of empathy. She tried to say that the last thing in the world she'd wanted to do was hurt you, and that she felt terrible about it. That's the thing with Maggie; you start out being mad at her and end up feeling like a jerk because she's so damned honest."

"She wasn't all that honest with me. You think it was honest to start sleeping with her ex-lover?"

"You don't know they slept together. You assume that."

"Damn right I do."

Martha let out a chuckle. "Just keep that anger, babe, and you'll be okay. You find yourself starting to slip, call me."

Finally, I gave in and laughed. "Martha, I know what you're up to and it isn't working."

"What?" Her voice was full of innocence.

"Your whole goal in life is to get me back together with Maggie Carradine. You think I suddenly buy this new reverse psychology?"

"I don't know what you're talking about." But her laughter gave her away. "I'll tell you one thing, though. I don't like the sound of this whole mess and that's the truth. I wish you'd at least give me some names or the details of these deaths. I could ask a few questions, see what I can find out."

"I promised her, Martha. No cops. If I gave you the names of the clients, just so you could run a background check for me, you'd have to promise not to do anything else with the information."

Now she really laughed. "You're a piece of work, you know that? You want to use my resources but not let me do my job. If I didn't love you, I'd be offended."

"But you do love me," I said, laughing too. "Have you got a pen?"

Afterwards, we allowed ourselves a few minutes of small talk and she invited me to have dinner with Tina and her. I gladly accepted and promised to bring Tina's favorite Cabernet.

After breakfast, I checked my e-mail. To my surprise, there were three messages. The first one wasn't very helpful.

"Dear Just Curious. Hope you dream of me tonight. If it turns out to be true, you'll be the first to know. Love, Studly."

I thought about referring him to the Cowgirls in Search of Studs on Steeds, then erased the message. Now I knew why people didn't give out their e-mail addresses, I thought. The second one was a little more useful.

"Hi, J.C. I'm P.J. (short for Psychic Junkie). If what you're describing is true, you're pretty special. But don't freak out. You're not the only clairvoyant in the universe. In fact, WE ARE EVERYWHERE. Does this only happen when you dream? If so, my guess is that you've got too much noise in your head during the day. You've got to clear the waves, darlin'. Learn to listen. If you're interested, I can help. E-mail me."

I copied the e-mail address and saved the message, then read the third.

"Just Curious? I don't think so. If you're having

dreams that portend the future, you're way beyond curious. But I'm definitely curious. How long has this been going on? Do you know it's a premonition when you wake up, or only after it comes true? Are the dreams exactly like what happens, or just a close approximation? How do you feel about the dreams? Are the things you dream about emotionally charged events? Traumatic in nature? Or are they everyday run-of-the-mill stuff? Tell me more and maybe we can 'connect.' Call me Claire."

Cute, I thought. As in Claire Voyant. But I saved the message and e-mail address. Of the two good responses, I felt Claire's was the most promising. The questions she asked seemed to indicate she knew a lot about the subject. I decided to concentrate on her.

"Dear Claire," I wrote. "Thanks for getting back. I hope you're not too disappointed to discover that I'm writing on behalf of a friend. To answer your questions, this just started a few weeks ago. There have been two dreams that have 'come true.' The dreams are very intense and violent. My friend has no idea that they're premonitions until the events have actually occurred. She says the dreams are almost identical to the actual occurrence. She has never been clairvoyant before, but she's always been a little psychic. Why is this happening now?"

I sent the message, then debated calling Maggie to fill her in. After five minutes of deliberation, I punched in her number. This time, she answered her home phone.

"Oh, hi. How'd the chat group go? Did you learn anything useful?"

"Well, sort of. No one was actually chatting when I tried but I left a message on the bulletin board and a couple of people responded. Three, actually." I told her about the message from Studly and she laughed. "I just want to find out more about what you're experiencing, Mag. Did you have any more, uh, dreams? And did you get hold of Stella Cane?"

"No to both questions. As far as the dreams go, it's getting so that I'm almost afraid to fall asleep. But after talking to you yesterday, I feel a lot better. At least I'm not in this completely alone. I know I already thanked you, but . . ."

"It's okay, Maggie. I wouldn't want you to be going through this alone, either. I mean, I wouldn't want anyone to have to."

There was an awkward silence and I was relieved when her phone beeped, indicating a call on another line. I hung up hastily, cursing myself. *Keep it professional*, I chastised myself. But even as I said it, I felt the little nugget of anger I'd been harboring begin to unfold.

Chapter Four

Stella Cane lived in Eugene, only a couple of hours from Cedar Hills. She hadn't been back to therapy since the day after her boyfriend's murder, and neither Maggie nor I had any luck reaching her at the number listed in her file. Had the police arrested her? Had she fled the country? Or maybe she just wasn't answering her calls. I didn't have any contacts in the Eugene Police Department, and I didn't want to involve Martha any more than I already had, so I decided to pay Stella Cane a visit myself.

One of the first things I'd learned about disguises

was to keep them simple. My old mentor, Jake Parcell, had taught me that, saying that most folks tended to overdo it, making themselves stand out like sore thumbs. "If you're blond," he explained, "why on earth would you switch to black hair? It don't match your eyes or skin coloring one whit. If you've got skinny arms and legs, don't try to make your tummy fat. It doesn't work. Go with what you got and just rearrange it enough to throw people off. Create an image and step into it."

And so I had. Though I rarely found the opportunity to use it, I kept a simple disguise handy for situations like this.

My natural hair is blond and short, making me appear younger than my thirty-three years. By donning a strawberry-blond, softly curled wig, I instantly aged about ten years. The wig was an expensive one and looked natural on me, though I didn't look a thing like myself in it.

I don't wear glasses, so the inexpensive pair I'd picked up at the drugstore further changed my appearance — not radically, but enough to alter the image. The round lenses de-emphasized my cheekbones, giving me a matronly look. I never wear makeup, so a touch of pink lipstick was enough to give the impression of a made-up face. A pair of earrings I wouldn't be caught dead in and a god-awful lime-green flowered jacket that was actually in style, completed the image. I was rounder, softer and older. I felt ridiculous, but the hideous jacket successfully concealed the thirty-eight tucked inside my shoulder holster, and the first time I'd worn the disguise, I'd walked right by Martha Harper and she hadn't recognized me.

I added the finishing touches using the rearview mirror in my black Jeep Cherokee, then headed toward Eugene. While I drove the two-lane road that wound its way through the evergreens, I thought about the best way to approach Stella Cane, if indeed I could find her. I had half a dozen cards printed up with various names and occupations. I could be Mary the Reporter, Dee Dee the Social Worker or Wanda the Realtor, none of which promised to do much good in this case. I'd have to go with Jane the Private Investigator, I decided. Not very original, but probably the best way to get her to talk, given the circumstances.

Compared to Cedar Hills, Eugene is a regular metropolis. Boasting a population of over a hundred thousand, it has a fine university, theaters, restaurants and the all-important Wal-Mart and Costco. The people are friendly, the streets are clean, and the air is a delight to breathe. Like most of Oregon, it rains like hell most of the year. But that Saturday it seemed the entire population was out and about enjoying the welcome April sunshine.

The apartment Stella Cane had shared with her boyfriend was outside of town. Using my Thomas Brothers map, I located Elm Street and followed a succession of increasingly dilapidated houses until I reached the shabby apartment complex bearing the address. Looking at the dismal surroundings, I wondered how Stella Cane had been able to afford Maggie's services. Therapy wasn't cheap. Unless, of course, Maggie was taking pro bono cases.

Rock music poured from an open window in the unit next to theirs, and a couple upstairs was arguing loudly. Number seven, however, was disappointingly dark and quiet. I knocked on the door anyway, then pushed my way through a thick hedge to the living-room window. I pressed my nose to the glass, cupping my hands to shade my eyes, and peered into the empty room. The place had been gutted. Not a stick of furniture littered the stained and threadbare carpet.

"You looking to rent?"

I wheeled around. Two beady eyes stared back at me from under a Forty-niners' cap. The man was pushing eighty, but his bony body had the wiry resilience of someone who'd worked long, hard hours all his life.

"I'm looking for Stella Cane. You know her?"

"The blond gal with the tow-headed kid used to live here? Sure. Poor thing had to move out, though. Her good-for-nothin' boyfriend got hisself killed. Police been all over the place asking questions and whatnot. Who knows? Maybe she done it. " His small eyes twinkled with merriment. "Why you want her? She done something else?"

"No, no. Nothing like that. I just wanted to see her. You know where she went?"

"Nope. I mind my own business and don't bother prying into anyone else's." He folded his arms across his bony chest as if to show me just what a stand-up guy he was. Since it had only taken him about ten seconds to spot me peering in her window, I had a feeling he spent more time than he cared to admit prying into his neighbors' business.

"You live around here?"

"Yep. That's my place, right across the street. In another month, them roses will be full bloom."

"They must be beautiful," I said. His kitchen window was directly across from where we stood. I wondered how often he'd stood there, watching the goings-on at number seven Elm Street. He must have read my mind.

"Can't say as I was too sorry to hear her boyfriend got it, though. He was a real nasty fella. Used to knock her around some, which I never could cotton to. He got what was coming to him, I'd say." He toyed with the bill of his cap.

"When did she leave?"

"Yesterday. She and another blond, looked just like her, they been piling stuff into a truck all week, load by load. Didn't have no man to help 'em either, though the other one, she was big enough to carry most the stuff herself."

"Did they say where they were going?"

"Didn't ask. Like I said, I mind my own business around here."

I did my best to suppress a smile and thanked him for his time. I'd passed a gas station earlier and now I headed straight for it, hoping the phone booth still had its phone book inside. It did.

If the big blond that helped Stella move out really did look just like her, there was a good chance they were sisters, I thought. Since there was no man helping them, I took a chance that the sister wasn't married. I looked under Cane in the phone book, crossing my fingers. There were twelve listings and ten of them were distinctly male names. One name, Toby, could have been male or female, and the other just listed the initial K. I tried that first and got a twelve-year-old named Katie who was very eager to chat. I tried Toby next and was rewarded with a husky female voice on the other end.

"Is Toby there?" I asked.

"Yeah?" She waited while my mind raced. The address was listed in the phone book. I could do this better in person than over the phone.

"I'm sorry. I must have the wrong number," I said, slamming down the receiver. I leaped into my Jeep, grabbed the Thomas Brothers and headed back to Interstate 5.

Toby's neighborhood was somewhat nicer than Stella's. The houses were old with little rectangles of untended lawns in front. Weeds poked through cracks in Toby's driveway and the house next door had a rusted Chevy truck jacked up in the front yard, one tire missing. I smiled at a growling black Doberman chained to a tree in her front yard and left him a wide berth as I made my way to the front door. The door was ajar.

"Hello? Anyone home?" I straightened my reddish wig and pushed the glasses up on the bridge of my nose.

The door creaked open a fraction of an inch and two dark blue eyes glared out at me.

"Uh, hi. I'm looking for Stella. Is she in?"

The woman snapped gum between her front teeth and continued staring. Her white-blond hair was tied back in a ponytail, revealing an oily forehead and pasty complexion. Her pinched features were not softened by the liberal use of eyebrow pencil and mascara.

"Who wants to know?"

"I'm Jane Oliver. Private investigator. Actually, I'd like to talk to her about what happened last Wednesday night. Are you Stella?"

I was pretty sure she wasn't. The woman Maggie had described was younger and more timid. This one looked like she'd as soon knife me as let me through the door.

"I'm Stella," a soft voice said behind her. Grudgingly, the woman moved aside to let Stella through.

Her unadorned face was puffy from recent tears, but her resemblance to the older woman was striking. With her shoulder-length blond hair, she was a kinder, gentler version of her sister. A child tottered behind her, his chubby fingers wound around the fabric of her pants. A fading yellow bruise circled his left eye.

"Can I come in? It won't take but a minute. Or if this is a bad time, I could come back." When Attila wouldn't be hovering over us, I thought. But Stella motioned me in and I followed her across the cluttered room to a checkered sofa. The room was in disarray with boxes piled on the floor and tables, but otherwise it seemed clean and well-cared for. A framed photograph was propped on an end table and I studied it with interest. A younger, beaming Stella was holding the baby in her arms, and a man I assumed was Hector stood behind them, his dark eyes glowing with obvious pride. He didn't look like someone who would beat his girlfriend and their child, I thought. But then, who did? He was short in stature and slight, with a pencil-thin moustache above gleaming white teeth. He wore his black hair pulled back in a ponytail and sported a gold stud in his left earlobe. He was dressed in a black silk shirt that looked more expensive than the clothes Stella wore. I tore my eyes from the photo and looked at Stella.

"I'm so sorry about what happened," I started.

"Who sent you?" Toby demanded. Stella sat on the sofa, pulling the baby up to sit in her lap, but the

31

sister remained standing, her arms crossed in front of her.

"I wish I could tell you," I said. "I've been hired to find out who really killed Hector and I, for one, don't believe either of you had anything to do with it. Let's just say that I'm here to help. I know how difficult this must be for you." I tried to project sympathy and competence at the same time. Hard to do with those silly glasses slipping down my nose.

"You're not with the cops, right?" the sister asked, looking me up and down.

"Right. Like I said, this is a private investigation."

"Good," the big woman said, her arms still crossed in front of her. " 'Cause those fuckers don't got no idea what's going on! Assholes tried to act like Stella had something to do with it. Not that she didn't have good reason to want that son-of-a-bitch dead. After what he done to her and the baby."

"Toby, no. Don't say that." Stella held her hands over the kid's ears, shooting her sister a pleading look. Tears welled in her eyes.

"Okay, okay. Don't start crying again, Stell. Let me take Junior for his nap. I didn't mean nothin' by it." She plucked the child from Stella's lap and carried him into the other room, crooning at him in a voice I'd have never guessed she owned.

"Don't mind her," Stella said, dabbing at her eyes. "She's just overprotective. How can I help you?"

"I'm trying to find out what really happened to Hector that night. I was hoping you could shed some light."

"I already told the police. He left the apartment about five-thirty for the Bird Dog. That's a bar he and his buddies always hung out at. I told him that if he

32

was going to get all drunk again to not bother coming home. Hector got nasty when he drank. I didn't want him hurting Junior. Anyway, when he stormed out the door, I made up my mind to leave him. After he left, I threw some clothes together and called Toby to pick me up. I didn't even find out what happened until the next day." The tears pooled in her eyes again, but she seemed determined not to let them fall. Like a woman who'd already cried too much, I thought.

"It was one of them drunken bums he hangs with, you ask me," Toby said, marching back into the room. "Guy I know works at the station said the cops found the bat in a dumpster about a block from where he was found, no prints or nothin'. And he was only a block away from the Bird Dog when someone got him. Probably pissed someone off in the bar and they followed him home. But the cops don't have nothin' to go on so they started harassing us. But Stella was with me the whole time and I'll swear to that in court. Plus, all anyone has to do is take one look at her to know she couldn't do it. Hector was strong, even if he was kinda scrawny. No way she could take him, drunk or sober."

Which was probably true, I thought. But Toby was a different matter. She looked strong enough and mean enough to take anyone she had a mind to. And she made no pretense of grief over Hector's demise.

"Did the cops say if Hector put up a fight, or if he was hit from behind?"

Toby frowned. "They weren't exactly giving away information. My friend at the station says it looked like someone jumped him, though. And it wasn't no robbery. His wallet wasn't even touched."

"Just the two of you at home that night?"

"Look, the cops already went over all that. What we watched on TV, what we ate, everything. I ain't about to go over it all again for some wannabe cop. You got a badge or something, proves you're who you say you are?"

I dug a phony card out of my jacket pocket and handed it to her.

"Big deal. I could get a batch of these made up myself." She smacked her gum, bright eyes boring into mine.

I moved my horrible flowered jacket back, revealing my shoulder holster, the thirty-eight tucked safely inside. Stella's eyes grew round. Her sister blew a bubble.

"Okay, so maybe you are a detective. I still don't know who sent you. Why should we tell you anything?"

"Because if you're as innocent as you say you are, then you should want whoever did kill Hector apprehended, right? Besides, the sooner I can find out who did it, the sooner the police will leave you two alone."

Stella looked at her sister, who shrugged her consent. "What else do you need to know?" Stella asked softly.

"Where were you two the day before yesterday?"

The women exchanged a glance. Toby stepped in before Stella could answer. "Let's see. Day before yesterday. That would be Thursday, right? Oh yeah. Me and Stella took the kid to the mountains just to get away for the day. We had the service on Wednesday and Stell was pretty torn up. We hiked around, had a picnic, like that. Later we got some more stuff from the apartment and came back here."

"Anybody see you up there? In the mountains?"

"Just the other people doing the same. Don't know their names, though. Why? What happened Thursday?"

From the look they'd exchanged, I had a feeling they knew exactly what had happened on Thursday. Somehow I didn't think they'd actually gone to the mountains. But had they been down in Gold Beach pushing an old man over a cliff? Or was there something else going on? I felt sure there was something they weren't telling me. Was it possible that after killing Hector, the two of them had conspired to kill Maylene MacIntyre's grandfather to deflect attention away from the first murder? Or maybe they'd made a pact to kill all the evil-doers in the world, starting with the ones they knew about. I looked at Stella's doe-like eyes and doubted she could kill a fly. I looked at Toby and knew anything was possible.

"What if I told you the police had proof that you didn't go to the mountains on Thursday?"

"I'd say you were lying." Toby smirked. "We were there, weren't we, Stell?"

"What kind of proof?" Stella asked.

"Let's say someone saw you somewhere else entirely. Got your license plate and everything. It doesn't do you a whole lot of good to lie. See, the police are funny that way. They think if you lie about one thing, you're just as likely to lie about another. Then they start thinking you're lying about everything." Kind of like I was.

"We didn't go to the mountains," Stella blurted.

"Shut up! Damn it, Stella, I swear to God!" Toby spit the gum into her palm and heaved it into an empty box on the floor.

"If I'm going to help you, I need to know the truth." I trained my eyes on Stella, ignoring Toby's clenched fists.

"I — I did something I shouldn't have." She looked at Toby, who rolled her eyes. I nodded encouragement. "I took something that Hector had, that was worth some money, and I — I sold it. I mean, I didn't know he was selling, I swear. But when I found it, what was I supposed to do? Tell the police? Flush it down the toilet? He didn't leave me and Junior anything. Nothing! He was gone and we didn't have anything. And then I find this big stash! I swear, I knew he got high, but I had no idea he was selling. Then I started thinking, if that's all Hector could leave his son, who am I to deprive him of it? You saw him, ma'am. You gonna tell me Junior doesn't deserve a break? You gonna tell me that?"

No, I wasn't. "Was this here in town? Or over on the coast?"

Toby narrowed her eyes. "The fewer details you know about that, the better. She shouldn't have told you in the first place. If you're finished, I'll walk you out."

Subtlety was not Toby's forte. She led me outside and when the Doberman saw her, he began straining against his leash, wiggling his rear and whining for her attention.

"See you around, detective," she said, snapping a new piece of gum between her front teeth.

"Take care of your sister," I said. We exchanged a grimace that no one would've mistaken for a smile. I didn't trust Toby any more than she trusted me, but I was glad Stella had her.

Chapter Five

Driving back along the Umpqua River, I watched great blue herons cruise the banks, their ungainly wings flapping inches above the surface as they scanned the depths below for an early supper. Occasionally an osprey would plunge into the water from high above, reemerging with something clutched in its talons.

I listened to a Tracy Chapman CD and sang along, the open windows blowing my hair while the afternoon sun warmed me. I'd stowed my gun and disguise in the back and it felt good to be in my own clothes.

Still, I was glad I'd worn the disguise. If Stella ever returned to the therapy sessions, I was pretty sure that she wouldn't recognize me.

I hadn't learned much from visiting them though, and I couldn't eliminate either one as suspects. I could picture big Toby with a baseball bat. In fact, I could imagine the whole scene. Stella calls Toby, in tears and finally ready to leave the asshole before he comes home drunk again and takes it out on her and the kid. Toby gets ticked off, decides to deliver a message to Hector herself, let him know he's not welcome in her sister's life anymore. She waits for him outside the Bird Dog and follows him down the street. When she finally confronts him, he gets abusive, calls her an ugly whore or something equally charming. Maybe Toby's brought the bat, just in case, to scare him. And since she's got it in her hands, she takes a swing. Maybe not to kill him, but just to let him know she's not a pushover like her sister. Only the bat meets his skull and he goes down. And then, maybe she can't stop herself and she just keeps swinging the bat. When she sees what she's done, she has the presence of mind to wipe her prints off the bat and toss it in a nearby dumpster.

I freeze-framed the image and shook my head. No way Toby would've had the presence of mind to do that. She'd have been in a rage, out of her mind. She'd have blood on her. She'd be worried someone would see her. And where was her truck? Back at the Bird Dog? Or maybe she'd parked it down the street and waited for Hector to walk by. Maybe the whole thing had been premeditated. But Toby didn't seem like the pre-meditative type. I could picture her swinging the bat, full of rage, out-of-control. But I couldn't see her wiping her prints off the bat. Someone more in control had done that. Stella? Had Stella been with her? Waiting in the truck? No way. Stella loved the bastard. The question was, did she love her sister more? Would Toby kill to protect Stella? Possibly. Would Stella help cover up the crime to protect Toby? If not, who had wiped the prints off the bat?

By the time I reached the coast, I was famished. Since it was too soon to join Martha and Tina for dinner, I checked the list of Maggie's clients, remembering that one of them lived on a boat somewhere on the harbor. Sure enough, a Donna Lee Kramer had listed her address as the *Sea Gypsy* on Harbor Drive. Just a stone's throw from Martha's harbor-view condo. I headed in that direction.

The Harbor Marina sat at the end of Harbor Drive, a string of cement docks hosting an assortment of fishing boats, tugboats, yachts and dinghies. Quite a few of the vessels looked lived-in. I parked in the lot, pulled on a Seahawks cap and got out to stretch my legs. Since I didn't plan on actually talking to Donna Lee, I felt I could forgo the wig and glasses.

I found the *Sea Gypsy* moored to the third dock. It was a teak and brass schooner that was easily one of the nicer boats in the marina. It had a decidedly feminine touch, with geranium pots lining the dock, a black-and-white tomcat sprawled along the wooden bow, and a string of newly washed laundry dancing in the breeze between the mainsail mast and the jib.

In stark contrast to the sleek craft, there was a stubby fishing vessel tied up in the slip next to hers. A seven-foot, steel-gray shark swung slowly from a giant hook hoisted above the stern, and blood still dripped from its mouth into the water. A ruggedly handsome man in black rubber boots and waders was hosing off the deck with one hand, holding a Budweiser with the other. I watched as he drained the beer, crumpled the can and lobbed it at the shark. The can bounced off and fell into the water.

Just then an attractive redhead poked her head out of the *Sea Gypsy* and called out to the man that his supper was ready. He turned off the hose, popped open another beer and leaped onto the walkway between the two slips. Obviously, the fisherman was Donna Lee Kramer's boyfriend. I did a quick about-face and headed back to my Jeep before either one could get a look at me.

I spent the better part of the next hour at one of my favorite wine shops, replenishing my own stock and choosing a few nice bottles for Martha and Tina. Then, realizing I was almost late, I headed for their place.

Martha's condo overlooked the north end of the harbor. It wasn't really big enough for two people, and since Tina had more or less moved in, space was cramped, but it had one of the nicest views in Kings Harbor and they hated to give it up.

Tina brought me a glass of Chardonnay and handed Martha a beer, gracing us both with a kiss on the cheek. She was a strikingly attractive woman with ebony skin and short-cropped hair, walnut-colored eyes that gleamed and a contagious smile. Martha was smitten and had been since they'd met. They were emotional and physical opposites yet seemed perfectly suited. I thought of Martha as a lumbering, huggable bear, and Tina an exotic, elegant cat.

"Mart says you're seeing Maggie again?" Tina's

eyes were wide as she curled herself into the sofa. She caught my look at Martha and laughed. "Okay, so she didn't say you were actually seeing her. Something about working a case?"

I took the chair opposite and sighed. "I couldn't exactly turn her down, Tina. Did Martha tell you what it's about?"

Martha settled onto the sofa next to Tina and slid her arm around Tina's bare shoulder. "Just the dream part, Cass. No details, I promise."

"Do you believe she really is having premonitions, Cass? It sounds so strange." Tina sipped her wine.

"Maggie wouldn't exaggerate this. If she says she's had two dreams that have come true, then she has. But I don't understand it. I've connected with someone on the Internet who can hopefully enlighten me about how this stuff works."

Martha took a swallow of beer and sat forward. "But hasn't Maggie always been a little psychic, Cass? You two used to scare me with your mind-reading. I remember one time you were halfway to the phone before it even rang because you knew she was calling. And she always seemed to know when you were thinking about Erica Trinidad. Remember how that ticked you off?"

I remembered. I also remembered how Maggie knew when I was thinking about *her*. That slow smile would start at the corners of her mouth and she'd look right through me until I blushed. Thinking about it now, I blushed and hoped to God that Maggie, wherever she was, wasn't picking up on my thoughts.

Martha picked up on it right away and chuckled, then graciously changed the subject. She said to Tina, "Is that the bread I smell?"

41

"Oh, damn!" she said, leaping off the sofa and running for the kitchen.

Martha chuckled. "Ran a check on those names you gave me. Only one came back with priors. Harold Bone had a couple of assault and battery charges about ten years ago right over the hill in Riverland. Although in both cases the charges were dropped. Seems both times, it was more the other guy's fault than his, according to witnesses. Even the bartender at the second scene said, and I quote, 'The dude he decked had it coming.' "

"Hmm. I suppose one could say that in the two cases I'm investigating, the victims 'had it coming,' too. Why were the charges dropped?"

"Doesn't say. Either both guys had a change of heart once they sobered up, or someone persuaded them to drop charges. It wouldn't be the first time someone was intimidated into doing that."

"What else do you know about this Harold Bone?"

"Not much. D.O.B. makes him right at forty. Occupation is construction worker. Six foot even and pushing two hundred pounds. Still lives in Riverland. Newly married last year. That's about it."

I pictured the man she was describing — a big, strong local boy prone to occasional bursts of violence — and wondered what he was doing in Maggie's group for victims of abuse. It was hard to imagine.

Tina called us into the kitchen where we began assembling shish kebobs. We skewered chunks of teriyaki chicken, mushrooms, pineapple, cherry tomatoes, red onions and bell peppers onto wooden stakes while Tina told us the latest courtroom gossip. She was a fledgling defense attorney and the only

African-American lawyer in Kings Harbor. She and Martha had yet to oppose each other in court, although they both knew the day would come when Martha would have to testify for the prosecution in a case that Tina was defending. It was just too small a town. They said it would be the ultimate test of their relationship and Tina swore that if she could sit and listen to Martha testify without sticking her tongue out at her in court, she'd bite the bullet and move in with Martha officially. Until then, they were, as Tina put it, just living in sin.

While Martha went out on the balcony to tend the grill, Tina pulled me aside. "You doin' okay?"

"You mean with Maggie? I think so. I don't know, Tina. I'm still so angry I can hardly look at her. But part of me wants to understand."

"That's 'cause part of you's still in love with her."

I shot her a worried glance and she laughed.

"Damn, girl. You think I'm blind? You got that look written all over your face."

"I do not. What look?"

She laughed again. "That one, right there. The one that says you'd take her back in a heartbeat if it weren't for your damned foolish pride."

"You think I don't have a right to be mad?" I was getting mad at Tina, just thinking about it.

"Oh, you got a right. She broke your heart and messed with your mind and all but trampled your pride. And she did it in a way that made her look like a saint because she was off doing a good deed for some dying woman and who's gonna blame her for that? 'Course you gotta right to be mad. You'd be a damned fool if you weren't."

"Tina, give me a break. First you talk about my 'damned foolish pride' and then you say I'd be a 'damned fool' if I wasn't mad."

"Kind of damned if you do, damned if you don't, huh?" She threw back her head and roared. Despite my irritation, I laughed too.

"Why am I laughing?" I asked.

"Because you know instinctively that somewhere in there I just told you a big ol' truth. Soon as you figure out what it is, you're gonna be just fine."

I was still frowning at her when Martha brought in the shish kebobs. "Is my girlfriend flirting with you?"

"No. She's telling me riddles and making me mad."

"Yep. She's flirting all right. That's exactly how she won my heart. Same way she wins those cases in court. Must've been Confucius in a past life. Don't worry about it, kiddo. She's usually right. Trust me. Come on, let's eat."

I followed them into the tiny dining room and looked out at the harbor where a tugboat chugged back to port. I felt oddly at peace. Something in what Tina had said made me feel better. I didn't know what it was yet, but I trusted that in time, I'd figure it out.

Chapter Six

On Sunday morning I had e-mail from both Claire and Psychic Junkie. I read Claire's first.

"Just Curious, I'm sorry to hear you're not psychic yourself. Your friend has probably just experienced some traumatic event that jarred this new ability loose, so to speak. Plenty of people have the power to 'see' and never exercise it. Right now, it sounds like she fears this new power because she can't control it and doesn't understand it. She is probably most receptive in her dream state, which is why she is 'seeing' the events in that state. This does not mean she is really dreaming them, however. She may be 'seeing' them as they occur, before they occur or even after they occur. Do you know which? Let me know, or have her ask me herself! I love to chat with other 'see-ers.' Fondly, Claire."

It was a good question. Was Maggie "seeing" these things before, during or after they happened?

Psychic Junkie was miffed.

"Hey, J.C. What happened? You dissed me, darlin'. I'm like, wow, totally jazzed to find a potential soul mate and then — zip. Nada. You find a better offer or what? But listen. Something tells me you're not as psychic as you claim but more psychic than you know. Okay, it sounds crazy, but those are the vibes I'm getting. Am I right? I think I can help you. Talk to me! P.J."

A little thrill of fear rode up my neck. Psychic Junkie had nailed me. I'd claimed to be the one who was clairvoyant and somehow he/she knew I wasn't. But I'd also always felt I was more psychic than I really understood. Somehow, P.J. had picked up on this. But how? Over the Internet? I was intrigued.

"Dear P.J.," I wrote. "Sorry, no dis intended. You're right, it's my friend who's having these premonitions or clairvoyant dreams, or whatever they really are. I'm just trying to help her out. Why would she suddenly start 'seeing' things in her dreams? And what do you mean, I'm more psychic than I know? How psychic are you? — J.C."

I sent the message and before I could shut down, my e-mail message box beeped.

"How psychic am I? Primarily I'm a sender, though I can receive better than a lot of people who claim to be receivers. I don't mean to brag, but hey, if you've got it, flaunt it. Let's get on a private chat line and I'll show you what I mean."

P.J. gave me instructions and in a few minutes we were connected.

"See? Isn't this better? Now we can chat. By the way, you should never leave your e-mail address on a bulletin board. There are more weirdos on the Net than fleas on a dog's ass."

"Yeah, I've already heard from someone who calls himself Studly."

"Who hasn't? That creep is a perv! He's on every chat line he can find. Most people put an Ignore Message on his name. So, getting back to the point at hand, this friend of yours. Is she gay?"

"What? Why would you ask that?" My mind raced. Had I somehow revealed more than I'd intended?

"I'm psychic. I'm trying to impress you."

"I'm impressed." How could she know that? And why did I assume P.J. was a woman?

"I'm very sensitive to these things. You know the old saying: It takes one to know one. Does that answer your question?"

"What question?"

"You were probably wondering how you knew I was a woman. But you did know, didn't you? You should learn to trust your inner voice."

This woman was scaring me.

"Don't be scared. Like I said, I'm a pretty good receiver. And besides, you're easy. I'd love to see your aura."

"My what?" Jeez, was this woman coming on to me, or what?

"Sorry. That must sound like a line, but I mean it. Some people have totally awesome, multi-colored auras, and I'd bet yours is like that. You send off radical vibes."

"Listen, P.J. It's been nice chatting with you, but I've got to go. Thanks for your help."

"Ask your friend how she feels after the dreams. Is she afraid, or is she strangely satisfied? Just ask her." I'm not sure which of us logged off first.

After chatting with P.J. I decided what I really needed was some fresh air and a good hard work-out. I changed into shorts and tennies, and went out back to chop wood. Sometimes, the simple rhythmic motion of swinging an axe can be soothing and by the time I'd split enough maple branches into fireplace-sized chunks to last a month, I was drenched in sweat. My arms trembled with the effort and my back ached, but my mind was clear and I felt good.

I went inside to shower, then called Maggie and brought her up to date on my meeting with Stella and Toby, trying to assure her that my disguise would prevent Stella from recognizing me in the event she ever came back to therapy.

"This I've got to see," she said, chuckling. "Cassidy James with curly strawberry blond hair, glasses and lipstick. You really think the sister could've done it?"

I admitted I didn't know and told her my plan to drive down to Gold Beach to get a look at where Maylene's grandfather had gone over the cliff. I was glad when she insisted on joining me. It would be good to get her reaction and see how close it was to what she had dreamed. I told her I'd pick her up around noon.

Maggie's house was an old brick and stucco building overlooking the south end of the harbor. Her office was downstairs, her living quarters up. I let myself in through the office door and found myself looking at the rather attractive backside of someone bent over a broken vase. Yellow mums and water were scattered across the hardwood floor. When she heard me enter, she whirled around, an apologetic grin on her face.

"Hi. Can I help you?"

"Dr. Carradine's assistant, I presume?" I couldn't quite keep the sarcasm out of my voice. So this was Maggie's little assistant. Cute, perky and, unless I was losing my ability to tell, definitely gay. One look told me all I needed to know. She was dressed in baggy plaid shorts that reached her knees, high-top tennies and a tank top that showed off finely toned biceps. Her tawny skin glowed with health and she looked like someone more suited to working at a Girl Scout camp than in a psychologist's office.

"Yep, and you must be Cassidy. I'm Buddy. Dr. Carradine said you'd be coming. She's upstairs but should be down any minute. She's going to kill me when she sees what I've done to her vase. It's her favorite one."

I knew. I'd given it to her. "Here. Let me help." I bent down and gathered up the flowers while Buddy plucked the shards of glass off the floor.

"She tells me you're computerizing her files," I said. "That must be an overwhelming task." I was trying to be polite to the little twerp, but what I really wondered was what the hell she was doing working on a Sunday. Shouldn't she be in Sunday school or something?

"Yeah, but I like it," she said. "I'm good at nerdy stuff like that. I was a real dweeb in high school."

She did not look like a dweeb. And she smiled at me like she knew it. Suddenly, I thought of something.

"Uh, as a self-admitted computer-nerd, you wouldn't know how to put an Ignore Message on someone's name in a chat group, would you?"

"Are you kidding? I spend half my life on the Net. I know, I know. I need to get a life. But it's addictive. Any4way, I can show you in a flash. You in a chat group?"

"Sort of. I just joined."

"Well, rule number one is don't give anyone your real name. Number two, don't give out your e-mail address unless you really trust someone. You never know who you're dealing with, and if the person knows what they're doing, it's not that hard to get your real address and phone number from your e-mail."

I decided not to mention the fact that I'd already broken rule number two and that all the psychics in the Northwest now had my e-mail address, including the infamous Studly. I laid the vaseless mums on the polished-oak counter and followed her to her terminal. I watched with awe as Buddy's fingers flew over keys, punching in command codes.

"Okay. See this? Just go like this and, bingo, the guy's messages are forever muted. You can still tell when he's trying to talk, you just don't have to listen to him. Pretty cool, huh?"

"Very. Show that to me again, in slow motion."

She did. "What chat groups have you joined, if you don't mind my asking?"

Actually, I did. "Uh, I'm just browsing at this point."

The way her dark eyes appraised me, I could tell she knew I was lying. She stood up and we were suddenly face to face, closer than I felt comfortable with. She was a little taller than I, with a slight, boyish build. She was athletic and graceful, with dark dancing eyes and short brown hair. Not only was she cute, I thought, she was Maggie's type. It dawned on me that she was a younger, darker version of me. She graced me with a full-blown, radiant smile and I changed the subject.

"I understand you're a college student? What are you studying?"

"Just undergrad stuff so far. I'm renting a studio right across from the community college, trying to save up enough for Oregon State next fall. This job really helps, and it's close enough, I can ride my bike when it's not raining. Saves on gas. Anyway, I'm thinking I might like to be a park ranger. I know that sounds weird coming from a tech-freak, but I love the outdoors. You ever go whitewater kayaking?"

"You mean like over rapids? I'm more the still-water type," I admitted. I'd done my share of kayaking on the lake and enjoyed the quiet solitude, the chance to move through the water almost silently, communing with Mother Nature in a way not possible in a powerboat, but I'd never really been tempted to try whitewater kayaking. Unlike Maggie, who loved to climb mountains, scuba dive and bungee jump, I preferred the quieter sports.

"Hmm." She brazenly looked me up and down and I suppressed the desire to squirm. "You don't seem like the still-water type to me. Course, still waters do run deep, or so they say." Before I could decide whether she was flirting or just being catty, she grinned and added, "I'm teaching Dr. Carradine to kayak. Shoot the rapids on the Rogue. You should join us."

Well, wasn't that just grand. And cozy, too. Maggie's little assistant was really starting to get on my nerves.

"Oh, I see you two have met," Maggie said, coming down the hallway. She looked from Buddy to me and back again, and I could have sworn she blushed.

"Buddy tells me she's teaching you to kayak." I kept my gaze innocent, my voice neutral, but Maggie raised an eyebrow.

"Yes. Buddy's quite the whitewater expert. She was a guide last summer on the Colorado."

Buddy beamed, revealing perfect white teeth and two perfect crescent-shaped dimples. She couldn't have been any cuter if she were Donnie Osmond.

Maggie looked questioningly at the flowers lying limply on the counter and Buddy rushed to explain. "Sorry. It was totally my fault. Right after I finish this cataloguing, I'll go buy you a new vase."

"Don't be ridiculous, Buddy. You don't need to buy me a new vase. I have dozens." She walked to a cupboard and pulled one out, adding water from the drinking fountain. "And anyway, there's no rush on that cataloguing. Let it wait until Monday, okay? Why don't we all just call it a day."

Buddy, looking momentarily crestfallen, switched off her computer and started tidying up the desk. Finally, she turned off the light and followed us out the front door.

"See you tomorrow, then!" she shouted, apparently recovered from her brief depression. She hopped on a red ten-speed and swung out onto Highway One, heedless of the Sunday traffic.

"She should wear a helmet," Maggie said, climbing into the Jeep.

"I see your maternal instincts are kicking in. How old is she, anyway?" I gunned the engine and turned south on the highway.

"Believe it or not, she's twenty-two. Still going to college and working her way through the whole way. That's why she needed the job. She's a hard worker, probably worth twice what I'm paying her. And she's smart as a whip. A little too exuberant, perhaps. Sometimes I have to force her to go home."

"So I noticed. It's obvious she has a crush."

Maggie looked up sharply. "What makes you say that?"

"Oh, come on, Maggie. She's practically panting over you. The child is lovesick."

"She's hardly a child, Cass. And I haven't noticed any panting whatsoever. In fact, it seemed to me that she was looking rather intensely at *you* when I came in. Do you think we could slow down, please?"

I looked at the speedometer and took my foot off the accelerator. I drew a breath and we drove in silence.

Halfway to Gold Beach, I told Maggie about my two new psychic friends and relayed Psychic Junkie's last question.

"Why on earth would she ask if I felt 'strangely satisfied'? That is just too bizarre."

"I thought so too."

"No, I mean, because that's exactly how I felt. Not

later, of course, when I realized those things really had happened, but right after the dreams, there was this sense of, I don't know, accomplishment. How could this person know that?"

"She's psychic, I guess. She seems to know what I'm thinking and we haven't even met, except on-line. It's spooky."

"Maybe you should steer clear, Cass. She could be one of those weirdos on the Internet we always hear about."

"Just because she's psychic doesn't make her a weirdo, Maggie. You, of all people, should know that."

She sighed and patted me on the knee. "You're right. What did the other one have to say?"

Just that simple touch and my insides tumbled. "She wants to know if your dreams are happening before, during or after the actual event."

"That's another thing that's been bothering me," she said. "I assumed that my dream about Stella's boyfriend was a premonition. But Maylene's grandfather was killed during the day and I didn't dream about it until later that same night. So it's not really a premonition, is it? Did either of your psychics say why this was happening to me? So far, none of the colleagues I've asked has ever had any experience with this kind of thing." Her voice sounded like it was ready to break. I'd never heard Maggie so vulnerable.

"They both say you're probably more receptive when you sleep. P.J. says you've got too much noise in your head during the day to be aware of your powers. Claire says you've probably had a traumatic event that has jarred this new ability loose. She says you may not be dreaming at all, but rather 'seeing' while in the dream state. By the way, P.J. asked if you were gay."

"What?"

"She said it takes one to know one."

"Oh, great. So now your weirdo psychic is gay, too. What did you say?"

"Nothing. She was just trying to impress me with her psychic abilities, I think. She said the same thing you said the other day — that I was easy to read."

Maggie laughed. "Well, she got that one right. You looked like you were ready to strangle Buddy. Your face is an open book."

"I just found her annoying, that's all."

"Bullshit, Cassidy. You found her charming and irresistibly cute. Like you. And you're jealous as hell."

I was speechless. I opened my mouth to say something and nothing came out.

Maggie laughed. Not unkindly, but it killed me. She went on, apparently unable to stop herself. "You see? Now you're mad. Because to admit that you're jealous is like admitting that you still care. And you wouldn't dare do that, would you?"

"Don't do this, Maggie. I'm really not ready for this conversation."

The tension was so thick I felt myself suffocating and rolled down the window. After what seemed an eon, Maggie exhaled.

"God, I'm sorry, Cass. I am so sorry. I have no right to speak to you like that. I — I can't apologize enough. You don't deserve that."

"You probably don't remember this," I said, my voice steely, "but you once accused me of thinking that as long as I apologized for something, it made everything okay. I've thought a lot about that since you left, and you were right. Being sorry doesn't negate the wrong. Not for me, not for you. Even if I accept your apology, it doesn't begin to undo the damage."

We both knew I wasn't talking about what she'd just said. The bigger issue hung over us like a cloud ready to burst.

"Again, point acknowledged." She sighed. "But just because you're not ready to talk about this doesn't mean I don't have something to say. I accept that you may not be ready right now, and maybe you never will be, which I'll just have to learn to live with. But I'm not going to pretend that there isn't something to discuss."

"Point acknowledged," I said, deliberately repeating her words. I couldn't bring myself to look at her. I could hardly keep the car on the road.

We drove in utter silence, the emotion between us so palpable I could feel it on my skin. Not until we saw the sign for Golden Estates twenty minutes later did Maggie venture to speak. "I think this is our turn."

I turned in, pulling up to an electric gate. I forced a smile at the uniformed guard in the booth, hoping he'd just wave us through without my actually having to speak, because I wasn't sure I was up to it. But it obviously wasn't my day.

"Can I hep you ladies?" His accent was straight out of the South. He was a beefy man with fingers like knackwurst, his palms the size of small hams. He crossed his arms and glared at us through mirrored lenses.

"Yes. We're here on the Ferguson investigation. I'm Cassidy James and this is my partner, Maggie Carradine." I handed him my real I.D. and hoped to God he'd think we were official.

"Private dick, eh?" He smiled and snorted. "Except I guess it don't exactly apply in this case, do it?" He was tickled to death by his own witticism and laughed so hard he started coughing into his fist. I'd heard it before. The dickless private dick. Maybe I should have it printed on a card, I thought.

"We'll only be a half-hour or so. The family just asked us to have a look. Not that they think the police aren't doing a thorough investigation. It's just that the granddaughter, she, well, sometimes people need to satisfy themselves with a second opinion."

"Maylene? Well, hell, why didn't you say so? I'm surprised she didn't mention it herself. She just left about an hour ago." He hiked up his waistband with his thick arms. "Tell you what. You-all just do what you gotta do and I won't mention nothin' to Officer Brown. Not that he would care, except between you and me, I think his feelings might be hurt, he found out Maylene hired an outside opinion. That ol' boy's been working this beat since she was yea high."

"I know what you mean, Officer Lewis," I said, glancing at his nametag. This always got them. Security guards are either real cops who have retired, or wannabe cops who for some reason never made it on the force. Either way, it was a safe bet to play to their ego. "By the way, you recall any visitors the day Mr. Ferguson died? Anything unusual?"

"Nah. I already checked the log. That was the first thing Officer Brown asked to see. Aside from the usual residents, we had a UPS delivery over to the Emmerson's and a realtor showing the Bernstein estate. Nothing else, 'cept for the gardeners, the mailman, the trash collectors and the folks who live here. Tell the truth, it was slower than usual. You wanna take a peek at the log yourself?"

"If you don't mind."

He thumbed back several pages and handed me a clipboard. Nowhere on the list for the date in question was the name Maylene MacIntyre. If she'd killed her own grandfather, she'd managed to get in some other way.

"What about this realtor, Agnes Mullholland? You ever see her before?"

"Not that I recall. We get them in here all the time, though, and the Bernstein place has been on the market since last summer. Half the realtors in town been over trying to show that place. I just have 'em log in like everyone else with the name of their office."

"This one says Twentieth Century. Was there a logo on the car or some other way to identify her as a realtor?"

The big man narrowed his eyes at me and hitched up his pants. "I didn't ask for no I.D., if that's what you're getting at. Like I said, these realtors are in here all the time. She had a client with her, another lady. They looked harmless enough."

"Can you describe them for me, Officer Lewis?"

His beefy cheeks actually turned pink and he coughed into his fist. "I'm usually pretty good at this, but I'm sort of drawing a blank," he said. "The truth is, except for the fact they was a couple of ladies, I don't recall them at all. Didn't make much of an impression, I guess."

"Who writes the license plate number in, you or them?" Since the printing looked suspiciously like that of the name, I feared I already knew the answer.

"Depends. Sometimes, I let them write it in, sometimes I walk around back and do it myself."

"And this time?"

He took the clipboard back and studied the writing. "Looks like they musta done it. Why you so interested in the realtor? You think she had something to do with the old man's death?"

"Probably not. I'm just thinking aloud. Is there another way into this place, other than this entrance?"

"Not unless you're Superman and can climb up the cliff from the beach." He chuckled, and leaned down into the car. "You want my opinion, the old geezer wheeled himself off that cliff. Not a lot to live for anymore. Even Maylene, who spent half her childhood here, didn't come to visit him, and the poor bastard didn't have a friend left. All that money and what good did it do him? In the end, he was just a lonely old man with no one to talk to."

I thanked Lewis for his help and drove through the electric gate, knowing that if I could get in that easily, so could someone else. Had Stella and Toby driven here, pretending to be realtors? Had Maylene donned a disguise and come to kill her grandfather?

"This is it," Maggie said. "My God, it's just like my dream."

I pulled up to the curb and we climbed out, taking in the view. Another electric gate blocked the drive, and the wrought iron bars were too closely spaced for either of us to squeeze through. I clasped my hands together in a makeshift stirrup and boosted Maggie up and over the gate.

"That's great, Cass. Now how are you going to get over?"

I jogged over to my Jeep and backed right up to the gate. I hooked a rope to my trailer hitch and tossed it over the gate. Then I climbed onto the hood, crawled onto the roof and catapulted myself over the gate. "So much for security." I grinned. "We'll use the rope to hoist ourselves back over."

The grounds of the Ferguson estate were soft rolling lawns sloping toward the ocean. The house itself sported white marble pillars, widecovered porches and picture windows overlooking the surf. A winding cement pathway bordered by red begonias wound its way to the cliff's edge where Maynard Ferguson had met his demise. As we neared, Maggie pulled back, her hand pressed against her chest.

"I don't know what I expected," she said at last. "It's like I was really here. Like I was the one who pushed him over." Tentatively, she inched forward, peeking over the side of the cliff to the rocks below, as if afraid the body might still be there. It wasn't. There was no sign that it ever had been.

"That guard was right about one thing. It would take an experienced rock climber to get up this cliff from down there," she said.

"Yes, but it isn't impossible. You could do it. So could I with the right equipment." I walked the perimeter of the fenced-in property, noting several places a person in fairly good shape might be able to climb over from the neighboring estate. Once they got past Lewis it wouldn't be too difficult for someone to get onto the Ferguson property.

The front door was locked and though I had my picks, I didn't think there was much point in breaking and entering. If there really had been a killer and he'd left a clue, it wouldn't be in the house anyway. It would be outside, long since trampled by the police and family members.

"Show me where you were standing, before you pushed him over."

"Cass! I didn't push him!" Maggie looked stricken.

"In the dream. You know what I mean."

We walked back down the cement pathway and Maggie stopped under a towering cedar. "I was here. Just behind that tree, I think. I waited for him to go by. He wheeled himself to the cliff and then I tiptoed up behind him." Her eyes were trance-like, deep in memory. I bent over and examined the area around the base of the tree. What was I hoping for? That the killer had left a note? A cigarette butt? A shoe-print? The fine bed of green and golden needles beneath the tree seemed undisturbed. I circled the tree slowly, and then something caught my eye.

"Look at this," I said, pointing to three tiny slash marks about knee-level in the bark. Two of the marks were horizontal, connected by a third that ran between them at an angle. "What do you make of this?"

"The number two?"

"Maybe. They were made with a penknife, it looks like. And it's recent, Maggie. Think hard, was this in the dream?"

"I don't know, Cass. I don't think so." As if trying

to summon the memory, she kneeled next to the tree and studied the marks. She shook her head.

"Okay, forget the marks for a minute. Did you have on gloves, Maggie?"

"I don't know. I can't see myself. Only what's in front of me."

"Shoes? Can you see your shoes?"

"I don't know!" Her voice was close to breaking and I realized just how upsetting this must be for her. I led her back to the Jeep, wondering why the killer would leave us a sign, if indeed that's what it was. And if he had left a sign, why so small and out-of-the-way? There were just so many contradictions. Number two? Had there been a number one at the scene of Hector's murder? Had there been other signs I didn't know about? I'd have to find out.

On the way back to Kings Harbor, I quizzed Maggie about Harold Bone, the therapy group member with the prior assault and battery charges.

"Think he could climb up that cliff?" I asked.

"I don't know, Cass. He's a big guy, but not in the best physical shape. He's strong, but not that agile. Why?"

"And this guy was abused by someone? As a kid?"

I could feel Maggie's gaze on me while she decided how much to divulge. "Well, I guess you'll find out in therapy anyway. Harold's father was a horribly abusive man. He liked to use his fists, his belt, whatever he had handy. Harold still has the scars to prove it."

I told her about Martha's background check. "You think Harold has adopted some of his father's tendencies?"

"Unfortunately, that wouldn't be unusual at all. He

hasn't mentioned it, though. I didn't know about the arrests. What happened?"

"I'm not sure exactly, but it seems Harold has a temper. Twice he's used his fists to take it out on someone who, according to witnesses, 'had it coming.' In both cases, charges were dropped, which is interesting in itself. Could be he threatened them into dropping charges. It's something to check out, anyway. I also find it interesting that he has a habit of beating up people who supposedly 'had it coming.' Seems to me someone could argue that Stella's boyfriend got what he deserved, and the same could be said for Maylene's grandfather. You think Harold might be playing vigilante?"

"I think it's possible that someone is. I really can't see Harold climbing that cliff, though."

"Well, the cliff is just one possibility, Maggie. Someone could've hitched a ride on the back of the trash truck. Or with one of the gardeners. They could've come in the night before, for that matter. Officer Lewis isn't exactly hard to get by."

When we reached Kings Harbor, Maggie offered to take me to dinner but I declined. In truth, I was starving, but the drive back had been too comfortable. It was just too easy to forget everything that had happened between us and to let myself slip right back into old habits.

I dropped her off at her place and sped back to the lake, eager to start compiling notes on my investigation.

Chapter Seven

Monday morning the sky was overcast and I could taste the threat of rain in the air. Panic had deposited a fat mole on the front step, meowing loudly for me to praise her. Gammon had turned her nose up at the sunless sky and had come back in to sit by the fireplace. I poured a second cup of coffee and logged onto the Internet.

There was another message from Psychic Junkie. "Hey, J.C. Didn't mean to scare you off yesterday. I just wanted you to know that you were dealing with the real thing. A lot of people claim to be psychic but they're pretenders. Posers, I call them. I wanted you to know I'm for real. I also think you are, too, even if you are calling on behalf of a 'friend.' "

I wondered about the emphasis on *friend*. Did P.J. assume that Maggie was more than a friend? Or was she implying something else? Maggie may have been right about P.J. being weird, I thought. I read on.

"So, did you ask her how she felt after these 'dreams'? Notice the quotes? That's because I don't think your 'friend' is really 'dreaming.' I think she's picking up on images while asleep. Anyway, I'm betting she felt a sense of satisfaction after the 'dream.' Am I right? I'll be in the chat room tonight at seven if you're interested in connecting again. Until then, stay dry! The weatherman says it's going to pour!"

This last note made me wonder where P.J. was writing from. I had purposely chosen a regional chat group, thinking if I narrowed it down to psychics in the Northwest, I might actually be close enough to one of them that we could talk face-to-face. I flipped on the Weather Channel and frowned. Rain was forecast along the coast from Brookings all the way to Seattle. Which meant P.J. could be miles away. Maybe it was just as well, I thought. I wasn't sure I really wanted to meet her. For some reason, I trusted Claire more. But Claire, apparently disappointed that I wasn't clairvoyant myself, hadn't left me a message.

Just for fun, I logged onto Psi-Chat Northwest and listened in. As soon as I entered the room, "Just Curious" appeared in an upper right-hand box listing the room's occupants. There were four other people in the room discussing something called scrying. From what I could tell, scrying involved objects such as crystal balls. I was startled when the one called Prophet addressed me.

"Just Curious, welcome. You have an opinion on this?"

"Not really. I'm just eavesdropping. I was hoping to learn more about ESP," I wrote.

The one called Leah answered. "Well, you're in the right place. What do you want to know?"

"For one thing, what's the difference between clairvoyance and telepathy?"

"I can answer that," Prophet replied. "Telepathy is knowing of events in another person's mind. Clairvoyance is knowing things that actually exist. For example, I tend to be telepathic. I pick up on what others are thinking. Very rarely have I had truly clairvoyant experiences."

Someone named Ra cut in. "I, on the other hand, am clairvoyant. I sometimes see things that are happening elsewhere."

"Can a person be both?" I asked. "And what if the event that the person is seeing hasn't actually happened yet?"

Leah answered. "That's called precognition. All three can happen simultaneously, though most of us aren't that lucky. But it's entirely possible for a seer to pick up on another's thoughts about an event that hasn't happened yet. Let's say Prophet is thinking about jumping from an airplane and I telepathically pick up on his vision. Later, when he jumps from the plane, my vision seems to have come true. But did I really envision the future? Or was I simply tuning into his thoughts about the future, which happened to come true? It's a shady area."

This brought on a whole flurry of conversation

which I could barely keep up with. Before I knew it, they were back to the merits of scrying and I logged off, shaking my head, wishing I'd taken notes.

Was it clairvoyance that allowed Maggie to "see" the murders, or was she telepathically reading the mind of the killer? And if her dream about Hector's death really *had* occurred before the murder itself, was that precognition, or was she just picking up on the killer's intentions? I felt like I had just scratched the surface of what portended to be a massive body of knowledge.

Regardless of how and why Maggie was witnessing the murders, assuming both *were* murders, the fact remained that the two people who died had abused Maggie's clients, which brought me right back to motive. Right or wrong, ever since I'd learned about Harold's previous attacks on guys who supposedly "had it coming," I had begun to think of the deaths as vengeful and the killer as some self-righteous vigilante. Somebody was righting wrongs. Or wanted it to appear so. It was equally possible that one of the murders was a deliberate attempt to divert attention from the other. But I had to start somewhere, and where better than with Harold Bone?

I checked the address that Maggie had given me. Harold lived in Riverland, less than an hour from Cedar Hills and only forty-five minutes from Kings Harbor where he worked construction. It was Monday and I assumed he would normally be working, though with the impending rain, it was doubtful the construction crew would be called out. Which meant I'd have to try him at home. Between now and our first therapy session, I wanted to get a feel for Harold's habits. In fact, I wanted to know exactly how and where he spent his off-hours, and to do that, I needed to crawl underneath his car. Not the easiest thing to do in broad daylight, I thought, but I had a better chance of finding his garage door open during the day than at night. If the garage door was closed, I'd have to hope for clear weather tomorrow and find his vehicle at the construction site. Either way, it was going to be tricky.

A few months back I'd had a case in which a woman who suspected her husband of having an affair insisted I buy a tracking device to keep tabs on her husband's comings and goings. At the time, I thought it an extravagant measure, but it did in the end save me a lot of wasted hours sitting in my Jeep watching his car from across some dimly lit street in the pouring rain. Whenever the man's Buick moved, my device alerted me to the target's direction and distance. If I were within five miles of him when he took off, I could usually locate the Buick by the time he had parked. If I was out of tracking range when he took off, it meant I'd have to crawl underneath his car later and visually check the compass transmitters to figure out where he'd been. This was a pain in the ass, but it prevented me from having to stay within the five-mile range all day. By the end of the second week, I could tell, without even bothering to follow him, which paramour's house he was either ap- proaching or had been to.

When at last I handed over photos to the wife showing not one but several different lovers, I was convinced of the tracking device's merit. Without it, I might have been satisfied after securing proof that he was in fact seeing someone, never to discover the extent of the man's infidelity. Unfortunately, I don't think the woman appreciated it quite as much as I did.

By the time I crossed the lake that morning, the rain had started to plunk down in slow, fat splattering drops. I pulled into my usual marina slip and tied up, ducking beneath the tin overhang. Tommy, the marina attendant, was down on the west dock, tossing a trout lure into the mouth of Rainbow Creek, which runs from the lake to the ocean a mile away. Shirtless under blue-jean overalls, he seemed oblivious to the weather change, but when he saw me, he came loping over, grabbing an umbrella out of his boat on the way.

"Hey, Cass. Better take this. It's starting to come down."

"Thank you, Tommy." I accepted the proffered umbrella and ran up the ramp to my Jeep Cherokee, jumping inside just before the heavens opened up.

It's an easy fifteen-minute drive to Kings Harbor on Highway One, but from there, the road to Riverland is windy and slow. Logging trucks, heedless of the rain-slicked surface, zoomed past me in the fast lane, but I was content to stay to the right, enjoying the sodden scenery. I'd seen enough slaughtered deer on the sides of roads like this to negate any thought I had of speeding.

Riverland is a picturesque town in the country, nestled between the North Fork River and gently rolling hills. I came here frequently, not for the ambience but for the outstanding French restaurant I'd discovered on the outskirts of town. Chez Suzette was so far off the beaten path, few people knew of its existence. But those who did came from miles around and were regular customers. As soon as I was finished with the task at hand, I intended to swing in for a late lunch.

Harold and his new wife lived along the river in an old, rambling farmhouse a few miles east of town. It was a semi-private lane, with just a half-dozen houses scattered along the south side, their rear porches facing the river. On the north side of the road, the ground sloped steeply up, so that the trees clinging to the hill arched over the lane, shading the farmhouses along the riverbank. It wasn't exactly the perfect place to set up surveillance, I thought. Even as I tooled idly down the road, I imagined eyes peering out at me from behind curtained windows. Luckily, every other person in Oregon drives a truck or sport utility vehicle, so I didn't exactly stand out.

Harold's place was near the end of the lane just before a curve, and I was relieved to see the garage door open. A green Ford pickup with mud-crusted tires was parked alongside a Volvo station wagon. A yellow and green tractor was nosed in beside the garage, under a carport out of the rain.

Because being a private investigator necessitates that I spend a great deal of time in my vehicle, I've managed to stock it with everything imaginable. In addition to a cache of food and water, I carry raingear, a flashlight, toilet paper, a wide-mouthed bottle (for those times when I can't get to a bush), a camera, binoculars, my Swiss Army knife, a fingerprint kit and a dozen other devices I've collected over the years. I even have an Insat wireless modem so I can use my laptop for faxing or e-mailing, no matter how far out in the boonies I might be. I've got a cell phone, too, but unfortunately, half the time it doesn't work when I need it. It's not the phone's fault. The problem is that the hills and mountains around that part of Oregon often block out the transmitters. Crossing my fingers, I punched in Harold's number as I rounded the bend and made a U-turn at the end of the road. I held my breath and hit *Send*, smiling when the phone actually rang.

"Hullo," the bass voice boomed. Bingo! The rain had kept Harold away from his construction job. I hung up and turned off the ignition. Now, all I had to do was figure out a way to get my tracking device underneath his Ford pickup, and I'd be in business.

The rain came down in a steady if unspectacular fashion, streaking the windshield, which didn't really matter because there wasn't anything to see. The curve where I'd parked was big enough to conceal the Jeep. Others had parked here before me, I noticed. It was either a lover's lane hang-out or a great fishing spot, because beer bottles and food wrappers littered the area. Which gave me an idea.

I crawled into the backseat and struggled into a full-length raincoat. I donned a pair of rubber boots and my Mariner's cap, then found the fishing pole I always carry in the back. All true Oregonians carry fishing gear in their vehicles. You never know when you're going to pass an irresistible fishing hole that no one else has yet discovered. A true fisherwoman would have probably had some nightcrawlers handy too, I suppose, but I wasn't that much of a die-hard anymore. I slipped the tracking device inside the raincoat pocket and stepped out into the downpour.

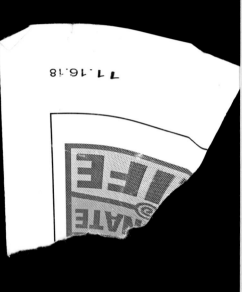

I made my way to the bank, slipping in the mud occasionally until I reached the river. To my surprise, I'd found what looked like the perfect fishing spot. The river rippled past a bend and tumbled into a deep, dark pool about twenty feet downstream. I wasn't in *that* big of a hurry, I told myself. I tossed a plastic lure with a barbless hook into the faster water and reeled slowly, letting the current carry the lure into the still, deep waters of the pool. To my utter amazement, the lure was hit. The line tightened and the little rod tip bent over nearly double. Line zinged out with a whine as I tried to tighten the drag. Before I could get my hand back on the reel, the fish jumped, a giant silver and pink flash of color arching gracefully above the water, twisting its sleek, impressive form with ease, spitting the lure back into the water before splashing back down into the depths.

My heart pounding, I stared at the water in awe. Probably the biggest natural rainbow I'd ever seen had just laughed in my face. I laughed aloud myself, glad I hadn't caught it, but grateful I'd been given the chance to witness its magnificence. Then I reeled in, secured the barbless hook to the eye of my rod and trudged along the bank through the rain toward Harold Bone's house.

Just for show, I tossed the line back into the water a few times as I worked my way along the slippery bank. When I got close to his place, I turned away from the river, pretending to fiddle with my lure. Though my head was bowed, I could see his back porch clearly. To my relief, both Harold and his wife were out back, safe from the rain under a huge metal awning, working on what looked like large, plywood Christmas decorations. It was only April, but the whole back porch seemed to have been turned into a Santa's workshop, and dozens of wooden cutouts were stacked on racks, awaiting paint.

I turned back to the river and tried to maintain a leisurely pace as I worked my way down river. I even tossed the line out a few more times, praying that nothing would bite. When I thought I'd gone far enough, I risked another look, then walked straight between their property and the neighbor's yard, back toward the road. No one stopped me. I looked like a tired fisherman, heading home for the day.

By now, my heart was beating rapidly, for I knew the next part was the trickiest. If either of them came out, I planned to use my knife to cut my hand. The sight of blood would help explain my presence in their garage. I could say I was going to ask for help. If Harold came out, it would ruin my cover as a group member later, but my hope was that they were too busy to come out and they wouldn't hear me because of the rain. And it would only take a few minutes.

I walked along the road, fishing pole tucked beneath my arm, fingering the knife in my pocket with one hand, readying the tracking device with the other. I reached their house, bent my head forward and walked purposefully up to the garage. Somewhere inside, a dog barked.

Damn! I rushed forward, slid onto my knees and pulled the transmitter out of my pocket. It was dark underneath the truck and my fingers were damp, making it difficult to get a firm grip. Finally, I heard the magnetic attachment click into place, and I breathed a sigh of relief. The barking grew louder, and I could hear his wife's voice coming closer, telling the dog to be quiet. I carefully slid out from underneath the truck, pulled open the blade on my Swiss Army knife and backed out of the garage. Not until I reached the end of the driveway did I turn around. If she'd come out, I'd have pretended to be walking toward her, not running away.

Once I made it to the road, I quickened my pace. By now, rain had trickled down the back of my neck and my cap was soaked, my hair plastered to my head. But Fido had quit barking and I made it all the way to my Jeep unchallenged. I knew that the tracking device was limited to a five-mile range, preventing me from monitoring his whereabouts from my home in Cedar Hills. Unless I wanted to camp out in Riverland, I'd have to spend a lot of time crawling under Harold's truck just to see how far and in which direction he'd gone. I only hoped it would be worth the effort. I entered my own mileage into a log so that I could precisely gauge the distance from his home to Kings Harbor, then set off for my favorite French restaurant.

It wasn't until I was safely away, halfway to Chez Suzette's and lazily replaying the scene in my mind, that something dawned on me. Mrs. Bone was pregnant. I wasn't sure what difference it made, but there had been no mistaking the subtle swell of her belly beneath her shirt.

The parking lot at Suzette's was empty and for a moment, I feared she was closed, but the orange and black OPEN sign hung in the window and the lights shone invitingly through the lace curtains.

Looking into my rearview mirror, I worked on drying my hair a little and thought about what to order. The house specialty, of course, was crêpes. My first few visits, I'd stuck with those, but over the past several years, I'd tried nearly everything on the menu, from appetizers of razor clams, calamari, or escargots to cream of morel soup, beef bourguignon and Suzette's favorite, her father's famed tournedos Richelieu with truffle sauce. She only made that dish once a year, on Bastille Day, and I hadn't missed it in three years. When I walked into the small, unpretentious restaurant, Suzette came scurrying around the counter to wrap me in a fierce hug.

"Where is everyone?" I asked. The place was empty. Not even the ubiquitous coffee drinkers who spent the day gossiping at the counter were in their usual chairs.

"Big Founders' Day parade in town. Been slow all morning. What are you in the mood for? You look like something the cat dragged in."

I ignored the comment on my soggy appearance. "What's that I smell?" I said, sticking my head into the kitchen. Suzette shooed me away with her dishtowel and waved me toward my favorite table.

"That's veal knuckles. I'm making a reduction sauce. You want a glass of wine while you wait? I'll surprise you."

These were words to make my heart sing. Not the wine, though her selection was astonishingly good, but the part about surprising me. There was nothing better than a gourmet chef in a creative mood, I thought, settling into the well-worn booth.

While I sipped the Bordeaux, I listened happily to the banging of pots and pans in the kitchen. Suzette sang loudly and out of tune while I tried to put together the conflicting images I had of Harold Bone. He was a big man, but certainly no body-builder. In his flannel shirt and coveralls, he'd looked like a friendly giant, towering over his pregnant wife, a slight, dark-skinned woman. They'd been working on Christmas crafts, of all things! Hardly the image of a vicious killer! But he'd been arrested twice for assault and battery. On the other hand, that had been ten years ago. He was newly married and his wife was expecting. People do change, I thought, finding the contradictions unsettling. To top it off, he was in a therapy group for victims of abuse. I was glad I'd finally get to meet him face-to-face the next day so I could see for myself just what kind of man he really was.

When Suzette finally emerged through the swinging doors, I was ravenous, which was a good thing, given the amount of food on the platter. Suzette set the food in front of me, then went to get herself a wineglass. She sat across from me and splashed wine into both our glasses.

"*Bon appétit,*" she said, smiling her gap-toothed grin.

"Like I've got any other kind," I said, already digging in. I'm not sure what all I ate, but there were black truffles on pork medallions, some kind of Alfredo sauce I could have cried over and something I suspected contained snails sauteed in garlic and butter. Once I got over the texture, and ignored the fact that the rain had brought out a veritable army of the little creatures who were at that very moment climbing over the begonias outside the window by my table, I admitted that the dish was to die for. Suzette does not believe in all the hoopla over fat grams, and it shows on her ample waist. While I ate, she regaled me with tales of her latest husband's gambling problem, and kept my wineglass filled, though I did my best to sip water now and then for good measure. By the time I'd finished, I was practically faint with happiness.

"Come back next weekend," she shouted after me as I made a mad dash through the rain for my Jeep. "I've got a big batch of chanterelles coming in!"

I waved, smiling at the thought of what Suzette would do with the wild mushrooms, and pulled back out onto the road.

Chapter Eight

Perhaps it was the wine and heavy French food that affected my dreams that night. Or maybe all the talk about Maggie's dreams had me paying more attention to my own. Whatever it was, I found myself sleeping fitfully, as if I were being yanked awake and dragged back down against my will all night. Finally, about three o'clock, I sank down into a half-sleep and watched myself participate in a dream I couldn't get out of.

The child curled herself into a ball like the kitten had done, back before the kitten had been thrown into the creek, its little head smacking against the boulder that had ended its suffering. The child did not want to suffer anymore. But she did not want to die. Not like the kitten.

She climbed into the trunk, thick with mothballs and must, burrowing down beneath blankets and cedar chips until she could scarcely breathe. Only then did the child allow herself to utter one deep but silent sob. Then she lay stock-still, holding her breath as the Bad One threw open the door.

"I know you're in here!" the voice bellowed. The stench of bourbon could not penetrate the thick planks of the trunk, but the voice was unmistakably drunken.

The child quivered, not daring to breathe.

"Come out now, and it won't be nearly half so bad." The voice was suddenly alluring, sweet, as the heavy body stumbled past the trunk. The child was not fooled. She had heard this voice before, many times, right before the fists flew, the eyes blazed, the real pain began. The child closed her eyes and prayed.

The Bad One clanged open the window, panting heavily. Then, with a curse-ridden shout through the open window, promising dire consequences if the child did not return that instant, the Bad One retreated, huffing obscenities under his breath.

The child stayed another two hours, barely able to breathe, suffocating under the heat of the quilts, but long enough for the Bad One to have sunk into the sofa, snoring himself into oblivion. Only then did the child dare to crawl out, hoping against hope that by morning the Bad One wouldn't remember.

I awoke, buried beneath my blankets, nearly suffocating from the heat. I threw off the blankets, surprising both cats, and got out of bed. My heart was pounding. The dream had disturbed me beyond reason. It was just a nightmare, I told myself. But I couldn't shake the feeling of helplessness and terror that the child had felt. Who was she? And who was the Bad One? They were both nebulous shapes, indistinguishable in their features. In fact, now that I thought about it, I wasn't even sure the child was a girl or that the Bad One was male. I closed my eyes, trying to bring their images into focus, but the harder I tried, the more they seemed to fade into memory.

I turned on lights and got the coffee going, though it wasn't quite morning. The cats joined me in the kitchen, suspicious about this change in schedule until I fed them. Then I set about working on my notes, trying to quell my uneasiness as I sorted through the facts.

It wasn't just Harold Bone I was anxious to meet. I wanted to get to know Maylene MacIntyre as well. Could she, after hearing that someone bashed Stella's boyfriend in the head, have gotten the idea to push old Granddad over the cliff herself? If so, the two deaths might not be related at all. Except that Maggie had dreamed about both of them. That was the problem. I could think of all sorts of motives and scenarios, but it always came back to this: Why in the hell was Maggie dreaming these things?

When the sky finally lightened enough to be deemed morning, I decided some exercise might help clear my mind. The cats followed me down to the dock and watched faithfully as I dove into the icy lake. I pushed myself hard, alternating between freestyle and the breaststroke, hugging the shoreline so as not to be mowed down by some early-morning boater. By the time I returned to my own dock, my chest was heaving but I felt decidedly better.

I let myself dawdle in the hot shower, then toasted a bagel, spread on a healthy dollop of cream cheese, and phoned Martha at the station.

"Hey, girlfriend. Today's the big day, eh? I can't wait to hear about your first therapy session with Maggie. Maybe you can reveal all your deep, dark secrets."

"Cute, Martha. I don't suppose you have time to do me another small favor?"

She let out her trademark laugh. "Since when do you ever ask for *small* favors? What do you need?"

"If I gave you the name of one of the people Maggie dreamed about, you know, that got killed, do you think you could get a copy of the crime scene report? I mean, without letting anyone know why you're interested?"

She laughed again. "I'm way ahead of you, Cass. You don't think I already figured out who it was? How many murders you think there've been in this part of Oregon during the last two weeks? Of course, I had to do a little guesswork. You gave me the list of clients, so I had their addresses. That helped. I ruled out a stabbing in Port Orford and a suspicious drowning in Portland. But that baseball bat thing over in Eugene sure caught my attention. Imagine my surprise when the vic's address matched one of Maggie's clients'."

"Martha, you promised not to interfere!"

"Who said I was interfering? I'll trade you."

"Trade me what?"

"I'll share what I know about Hector Peña's death

and you tell me who the other vic is. I've plumb run out of murders."

It was my turn to laugh. "That's because it hasn't been ruled a murder. The guy fell to his death. The paper said they were going to do an autopsy to see if maybe he had a heart attack or something. No one's mentioned a single word about foul play. Except Maggie, of course."

"That Ferguson guy? The rich lumber baron that drove his wheelchair off the cliffs down in Gold Beach?"

"Your turn, Martha. What can you tell me about Hector Peña's murder?"

"If you've got time for lunch, I'll show you what I've got."

I agreed to meet Martha for lunch, then went out back to work in my garden. I tend to entertain guests in the front yard because of the lake view, but my favorite place to be is in my backyard. My property is nestled in a valley and the ground slopes away steeply on three sides so that I'm completely surrounded by towering trees. Cedar, fir and blue spruce are scattered up the hillside but my favorites are the maple trees whose branches arch gracefully out over the yard. A natural spring that supplies my drinking water also feeds the creek that runs right through my yard to the lake. Along the creek, I've planted every imaginable flowering bulb, perennial and annual so that even in the dead of winter, flowers abound. Now, with spring underway, the bushes and clumps of green foliage were studded with blossoms ready to burst into color.

I walked past the hot tub on my back deck to the stream and pulled a few weeds along the bank, working my way toward the greenhouse at the rear of the yard. It hadn't taken me long to recognize the obvious merits of the greenhouse. I'd built it to trap as much sunshine and warmth as I could for growing herbs and vegetables. But an added bonus was that the deer, try as they might, couldn't help themselves to the fruits of my labor.

I noticed the unmistakable cloven hoofprints in the damp earth near the entrance and smiled. A doe and two fawns had paid a recent visit.

Inside, the air was warm and thick with earth smells. I checked the drip irrigation system, then inspected the tomatoes for signs of cutworms. So far, the foliage looked perfect and dozens of yellow flowers had already given way to tiny green fruit. By August, I'd have more tomatoes than I'd know what to do with, but right now I was impatient for the rich, warm taste of a juicy, ripe tomato right off the vine.

I moved toward the herb section and thinned out the parsley, grooming the chives, oregano and thyme as needed. It wasn't so much that my ministrations were required, as that the process comforted me. I liked to work my fingers in the dirt, breathing in the heady scent of the soil. I liked to imagine I could see the vegetables growing, and felt my presence somehow assisted their efforts. Often, I found myself talking to the plants, knowing it was silly but not really giving a damn. By the time I finished that morning, it was nearly noon.

I washed up, then rushed to meet Martha at a little Mexican restaurant called Pepe's, on the south side of Kings Harbor. It wasn't very long ago that you couldn't find a decent taco north of California, but recently that was changing. Pepe's wasn't bad, as long as you kept the order simple. We both ordered the number seven combination and Diet Cokes.

"You sure this won't ruin your appetite?" she asked. There was a yellow manila envelope on the table between us.

"Probably. But show me anyway."

"Officer Henzley faxed me these as a courtesy. I helped him out last year on a hit-and-run and he owed me. I'm serious, Cass. They're pretty gruesome. Ol' Hector probably never saw it coming. The first blow caught him behind the ear on the right side. From the angle, it looks like the perp's probably right-handed."

She slid a picture out and pushed it across the table. I took one look and closed my eyes to steady the sudden nausea.

"Thirteen times the perp made contact. M.E. report said Hector was dead after the third blow. I guess the other ten whacks were for punitive damages. Anyway, see this?" She slid out another picture and placed it on top. "Blood splatter everywhere except this spot here. The perp didn't leave any footprints in the blood. But the blood left splatter around the toe of the perp's right foot. That means the perp had plenty of splatter on the tip of his boot. At least they're guessing it's a boot. Not the pointy cowboy kind, but your basic rubber rain boot. Which indicates that the murder was premeditated."

"Why's that?"

" 'Cause it wasn't raining that day. Who wears rubber rain boots when it's dry outside?"

"Okay, I buy that. But why are you assuming it's a man?"

"Well, I'm not, really. Henzley is. From the toe it looks like the boot size is large."

"You wear a large," I reminded her. And so, probably, did Toby Cane. "I have a pair of large rain boots I wear over my tennies," I pointed out. "I don't think they should be ruling out a woman."

"There's also the fact that violent crimes like this tend to be more of a guy thing. This isn't just my opinion, mind you. Past history suggests that crimes of this nature are usually committed by males."

Martha slid the last picture out and handed it across the table. "Here's what I wanted to show you," she said. "Henzley thinks the doer started to write something. See that *N* right there in the blood? Could be nothing more than a couple of scuff marks, but Henzley thinks the guy, or *gal*," she said, looking at me, "might've been interrupted before he or she could finish whatever they wanted to write."

I stared at the three crude slashes, shaking my head. I turned the picture sideways and handed it back across the table. "It's not an *N*, Mart, it's a *Z*."

"What makes you say that?" she asked, looking at the marks now that the picture was turned.

" 'Cause they did it again at the Ferguson place. I thought maybe it was the number two, but I don't think so. I've got a feeling our killer sees himself — or herself — as Zorro."

Chapter Nine

I pulled into Maggie's parking lot just before three and parked beside Harold Bone's truck near the back wall. The Jeep would help conceal me, but it was still risky. I waited until Donna Lee walked into the office, then pulled a quarter out of my pocket and purposely let it roll underneath the truck. Quickly, I ducked beneath the back bumper and clicked on the digital read-out, noting direction and distance traveled. They were nearly identical to those I'd calculated in my log. It seemed Harold Bone had gone straight from home to work to therapy. So much for high-tech surveillance, I thought. I reset the device, then backed out, straightening my clothes before heading for the front door.

I couldn't believe how nervous I felt walking into Maggie's office. Buddy looked up from her computer quizzically. "Dr. Carradine's got a group session in a few minutes," she said.

"I know," I said. "That's why I'm here."

"Oh. Sorry. I thought you were here, you know, as a friend."

"Yeah, well. Even friends need help now and then. Is this where I sign in?" I indicated the clipboard on the wooden counter.

Buddy seemed as embarrassed as I was. "If you're a new client, you need to fill out one of these," she said, handing me a legal-sized form. "Most of the group's already here, in the waiting room. I guess you can finish the form afterward, if you run out of time. You nervous?" Her dark, dancing eyes appraised me and I felt myself blush.

"Actually, I am," I admitted. "Is it that obvious?"

"Well, basically everyone who comes in here for the first time seems nervous. At least you've been here before, though. I mean, since you already know Dr. Carradine, it should be easier for you. Right?"

I wasn't sure which was more unprofessional — the notion that Maggie would include me in her group, or that Buddy was so willing to talk with me about it. Maybe Buddy figured that if Maggie could break some rules, so could she. "Right," I said. I took the form and headed for the waiting room, wondering why Buddy's easy candor threw me off balance. Was it because, as Maggie had said, I was jealous of her? Or was it because in truth I found her just the teensiest bit attractive?

The waiting room was tastefully decorated in pale peach and green and featured an abundance of fresh-cut hydrangeas and live philodendrons. Maggie had a green thumb and it showed. It felt more like someone's living room than a therapist's waiting room, with comfortable chairs arranged in a U around a low square table covered with magazines.

Harold Bone was seated next to Donna Lee, the redhead who lived on the boat. They were both reading magazines, ignoring each other. Across from them, a slight, milk-complected young man sat nervously drumming his fingers on the armrest while he stared at the dark screen of the TV in the corner. His legs were crossed at the knees, and his foot tapped the air in rhythm with his fingers. This must be Joel Harris, the man who still lived with his mother, I thought. In Maggie's brief description of her clients, she'd painted the picture of an emasculated young man, who'd been teetering for years on the brink of suicide. When I entered, all three looked up then straight back down, as if afraid that eye contact might result in contracting something contagious.

No sooner had I taken a seat than Maylene MacIntyre entered. She was a tall brunette about Maggie's age, dressed in an expensive, dull-brown suit with shoulder pads that didn't quite conceal her poor posture. She had the stoop-shouldered slouch of a tall woman trying to appear shorter than she was. She glanced around the room, and when her gaze settled on me, she furrowed her brow. I smiled in what I hoped was a timid, friendly fashion and looked back at my form.

The last to arrive was Mrs. Bombay, an overweight, heavily rouged, dyed blond in her fifties. She was wearing a flowered pantsuit, the only piece of bright clothing in the room. She smelled of Chantilly, I thought. I watched as she promptly began touching up her lipstick. Except for Stella, everyone was present.

Maggie strode into the room and greeted the group with a warm smile. Nervously, we filed after her, past her office to the group therapy room where the chairs were arranged in a circle. They all seemed to know their place so I waited until they were seated, then took the chair that Maggie indicated. Stella Cane's seat was left empty.

"Everyone, I'd like to welcome Cassidy to our group. Why don't we start today by introducing ourselves?" This evoked the same enthusiasm as a dentist's drill, but they complied, mumbling their names while staring at the red Persian rug in the center of the circle. Only Mrs. Bombay gave her last name, oddly omitting her first, while Donna Lee ran her first and middle names together as if in one garbled sound. She smiled at me and I felt ridiculously grateful for the gesture.

Maggie crossed her legs and turned her attention to me. "Cassidy, let me tell you a little about how we work here. And make no mistake about it, it *is* work." This got a few nervous chuckles. "Each of us is here for different reasons, yet we share common experiences. Because of our shared experiences, we are able to help one another work through our own problems." A few heads nodded and she went on. "No one has to talk until they're ready, but we don't have time for B.S." This brought on some more laughter, and the climate in the room seemed to shift. I felt myself beginning to relax. "Anytime you feel like jumping in, feel free. And if what we're discussing seems too painful, feel free to say that, too. From this point forward, you're a part of this group. Everything we do here will be a group effort. And as you know, everything that is said inside this room stays here. Before we get started, we need to know if you accept these conditions."

I felt their gazes on me. "Yes," I said.

"And is there anyone here who doesn't feel comfortable accepting Cassidy into the group?" I waited, half-hoping someone would object to my presence so I could get the hell out of there. Only Harold Bone spoke up.

"Hey, the more the merrier."

"Thank you, Harold. Anyone else?"

"Let's get started," Mrs. Bombay said, smoothing her coiffed hair. "I don't think anyone minds one bit." She had a Southern accent and spoke with authority.

Maggie waited, and when no one else spoke, she went on. "Okay, that settles that. Who would like to start today? Mrs. Bombay, you had something to say?"

"I just wanted to ask Maylene how she was doing? Now that her grandpa's gone? I mean after what he done to her and all. I read about his accident in the paper. How you doin', doll?"

Everyone looked at Maylene, then to Maggie.

"For those of you who might not have heard, Maylene's grandfather passed away last week. Do you want to talk about it, Maylene?"

She shrugged. Her brown hair fell forward, partly concealing her eyes. "What's to say? I guess I'll be richer now." She looked around, as if to see what reaction her words evoked.

"You g-g-glad he's d-d-dead?" Joel asked. Maggie hadn't mentioned the stutter. The poor kid was in his twenties but seemed fifteen.

Maylene looked up sharply. "That's stupid, Joel!"

Joel immediately slunk back in his chair. Harold Bone spoke up, stroking his beard. "It's not really a stupid question, Maylene. I was wondering the same thing. When my old man died, I was as glad as could be. I know it sounds terrible, but it's the truth and like Dr. Carradine says, there ain't no time for bull-shit. The bastard beat me from the time I was old enough to crawl. I didn't shed any tears when he drank himself to death."

"She's not like you, Harold. Women are different." It was Mrs. Bombay offering this insight in her Southern twang.

"How so?" Donna Lee asked. Her flaming red hair was tied back in a ponytail and she was dressed in jeans and a sweatshirt.

"Well, look at you," Mrs. Bombay said. "When what's-his-name, Roy Boy, smacks you, you hate his guts, right? Ready to leave him right then and there. Then later he brings you flowers, talks real sweet, begs for forgiveness and wham, all your anger flies right out the door, right along with your common sense. If he ended up like Stella's beau, you'd be crying your eyes out just like she was. Women just don't know how to hate, that's all."

"Your mama sure knew how, didn't she?" Donna

Lee spat back. Silence flooded the room. Mrs. Bombay patted and smoothed the fabric of her pants before meeting Donna's gaze.

"That she did, child. That she did. But my mama weren't no ordinary woman."

"M-m-mine neither," Joel almost whispered. He threw a quick glance at Maggie.

"You want to talk about that?" she asked. Joel shook his head. Maylene started to cry and Maggie handed her a tissue. Everyone shifted nervously, eyes downcast.

Donna Lee finally spoke up. "I think I know how you feel, Maylene. Of course you hated him. You might have even wished him dead a thousand times. But you loved him in a way, too. Some people probably can't understand that, but I do. But it's okay if you do feel glad he's dead. That doesn't make you a bad person."

This brought on a new wave of tears and Maggie handed Maylene the box.

Harold was nodding his head. "Son-of-a-bitch had it coming."

"That's what you said about Stella's boyfriend," Donna Lee said.

"Well, it's true," he said. There was an awkward silence until Mrs. Bombay giggled.

"Ol' Roy Boy better watch his back," she said, smiling at Donna Lee. "The way things are going around here, it doesn't look too good for the bad guys."

"What's that supposed to mean?" Donna Lee asked.

"Well, think about it, darlin'. They're dropping like flies, ain't they? Maybe I better put in a call to the mental ward, see how my mama's doing. Maybe she choked on a fish bone or something. I can always hope."

"I th-th-thought you s-said that w-w-women don't hate."

"Oh, Joel, honey. That's regular women, not me. I was brought up by the master hater of all time. I learned real good how it's done. Why do you think I'm here? I'm trying to unlearn some of it, that's all. Take some of mine and give it to you-all." She winked conspiratorially at me. "How about you, Cassidy? You got some good ol' hate inside you? Or are you all torn up inside and too much of a wuss to get mad?"

I felt myself blush. "A little of both, I guess."

"Do tell," Mrs. Bombay said, turning in her chair to face me.

"Maybe she don't want to talk her first day," Harold said.

Everyone's eyes were trained on me. Even Maylene had quit crying.

I cleared my throat. "I guess I agree with what Donna said about being able to love and hate at the same time. If you love someone first, and then they hurt you, you don't just quit loving them, even if you get mad enough to hate them. It's complicated, I guess." I could feel Maggie's gaze as if it were fire and my cheeks burned.

An eternity of silence ensued. Finally, Maggie saved me by changing the subject. Gratefully, I sat back and watched as they took turns alternately knocking one another down and then helping one another back up. They were like sparring partners, I thought, dancing around tender topics, jabbing, but seldom hard enough to draw blood. Little by little, they were opening old wounds, and I reluctantly began to see the merits of group therapy.

Finally, Maggie told us that time was up. People looked up, as if surprised that so much time had already passed. I felt like we'd been there for hours. Maggie pushed back her chair and walked to the door, opening it wide. "Cassidy, you can finish that form in my office, if you like," she said, ushering us out.

As they filed past me, Donna Lee squeezed my shoulder. "Glad you joined us, Cassidy. See you on Thursday." For a brief second, I almost found myself looking forward to it.

I walked into Maggie's office and quickly filled out the form while I waited for Maggie to join me. When she came in, she sat down beside me.

"Well, what did you think?"

"Lots of emotion in there, that's for sure. Mrs. Bombay's a piece of work, isn't she?"

"Poor thing. You should hear her childhood stories. And poor Joel. I was hoping the others would help him open up, but I'm not sure it's working. That was about the most he's ever spoken."

"I take it his mother's the problem?"

"And he still lives with her," she said, nodding. She was staring at me intently. "You handled yourself pretty well, I thought. I think they bought it."

"Yeah, well. I had to think fast for a minute there. I wasn't expecting to talk."

"Well, you convinced me. Sounded like words straight from your heart." She let out a short, pained laugh.

"Maggie, don't. "

"We've got to talk about it sometime, Cass."

Before I could answer, we heard a shriek from the other room.

"Buddy!" Maggie said. We raced for the door.

She was lying facedown, sprawled motionless beside her desk. Another shattered vase littered the floor. The outside door was wide open. Maggie rushed to Buddy's side and I sprinted out the door to the parking area, looking frantically in all directions. Mrs. Bombay's station wagon was just pulling out onto the highway. It seemed everyone else was already gone.

Back inside, Buddy was sitting up, rubbing at the lump on the back of her head.

"You didn't see them?" Maggie was asking.

"I thought everyone was gone," she said. "I was bent over the filing cabinet and wham, I got whacked. Looks like I owe you another vase," she said, trying to smile despite her obvious discomfort.

Maggie pressed a tissue to Buddy's head and it came away red. "Let me look at that," she said.

"It's okay. Really." Buddy pushed herself to her feet, swaying a little. "Hey, I think they took the file."

"What file?" I asked.

"The one I was putting away. I'd just added your name to the group folder so I could put your form inside and now it's gone." She was looking around the room, but it was obvious the folder was missing.

"What was in it?" I asked.

"Well, the billing information, for one thing. And the original paperwork. Nothing special. I've got most of it on disk already. Damn, this thing is really bleeding." The new tissue was already soaked through and at the sight of it, Buddy started to sway again.

"Sit down," Maggie ordered. "Cass, come here. Do you think she needs stitches?"

I moved Buddy's hair aside, looked at the half-inch gash and nodded. "Come on," I said. "We'll take my Jeep."

Once we'd determined that Buddy wasn't going to bleed to death, Maggie let herself worry about the missing file. While Buddy was getting stitched up, Maggie walked me out to the Jeep.

"You think someone in the group took the file?"

"Probably. I saw Mrs. Bombay leaving in her station wagon. Everyone else was already gone. Or hiding," I added.

"But there's really nothing much in those files. Nothing confidential about the cases, at least."

"Maybe they didn't know that. Or maybe someone wanted your clients' addresses. Maybe someone's planning ahead for the next murder."

"Don't say that," she said. She was trying to sound brave, but her eyes told the truth.

"Hey." I grabbed her hand and held it with both of mine. Suddenly I was aware of how close we were, and how intensely we were gazing at each other.

Buddy's voice startled us both. "You weren't going to leave without me, were you?" she shouted, jogging across the parking lot toward us. Her hand was pressed against the rectangle of white gauze taped to her head, but otherwise, she looked quite cheerful. I dropped Maggie's hand and stepped back, acknowledging the slight smile that had passed between us.

"I guess you'll be headed back for the lake?" Maggie asked.

"Just as soon as I drop you two off," I said, knowing I sounded much more aloof than I felt.

Chapter Ten

The rain was at it again Wednesday morning. The sky was a dull gray for as far as I could see and the house was cold. I got the coffee pot going, then arranged kindling in the fire place. Once the flames took hold, I threw on a few logs, and poured myself a cup of coffee.

"What happened to spring?" I said grumpily to Gammon who was looking disconsolately out the sliding glass door. She meowed in answer and turned tail, heading for the laundry basket that I kept piled with towels for just such occasions. She leaped in, circled three times and then burrowed down inside the towels for the duration.

I hadn't had a chance to tell Maggie about the *Z* written in Hector Peña's blood. I hadn't told her I'd put a tracking device under Harold Bone's truck either. I picked up the phone and then, remembering the look we'd exchanged, hung up before I even dialed. Instead, I booted up my laptop and checked my e-mail.

Psychic Junkie had left me two messages, the latest a few minutes before nine. I checked my watch and realized that I'd just missed her. Apparently she'd waited for me to join her on-line last night and felt I'd stood her up. This morning, she said she had something important to share with me and asked me to e-mail her. What the hell, I thought. I wrote a brief note, telling her I'd been tied up with other things and asked what important information she had to share. As before, I'd barely sent the message before my own e-mail chirped. Apparently, either P.J. had access to a computer at work or she sat around all day at home waiting for e-mail.

"Hey, J.C. Let's get on a private chat line so we can talk! Same place as before. Meet you there! — P.J."

She was waiting for me when I got there. "Hey. Nice to see you!"

"Hi. You said you had something important?"

"You don't waste time with pleasantries, do you? Okay, but first, did you have a chance to ask your 'friend' how she feels after the 'dreams'? You did remember to ask."

"Yes. Like you suggested, she said she felt strangely satisfied. How did you know that?"

"Yes!" I could just picture her, wherever she was,

whatever she looked like, pumping her fist in the air. "I knew it!"

I wrote back, "I realize that. The question is, how did you know it? And why would she feel that way?"

"Because your friend isn't clairvoyant at all. She's telepathic. She feels what someone else is feeling. The satisfaction comes not from whatever she sees or, in her case, 'dreams,' but from what the other person, the sender, feels when they realize they've sent the message successfully. Do you get what I'm saying?"

"Not really," I admitted. "You're saying that someone is deliberately sending my friend these dreams? Can people do that?"

"Not many, J.C. Most people think receivers have the greatest talent, but that's because they don't understand what a really good sender can do. Imagine being able to project your thoughts onto someone else. To make them see what you're thinking, without them knowing that you're doing it! Mind-control experts have toyed with this for centuries, but of course, very few people have the advanced skills and natural talent to actually do it. What do you think the really talented witches and wizards were doing in the good old days?"

"How do you know all this?" I asked.

"I'm a sender, J.C. Like all good senders, I can receive a bit too. Multi-talented, I guess, though nowhere near as talented as your friend's sender sounds. I'd like to meet him or her. Any chance of that?"

"Sorry. I'd like to meet whoever it is myself. But I appreciate the info, P.J. You said you had something important to tell me?"

"It's just a premonition, really. Maybe nothing. I've had this feeling, though, ever since we started chatting, that your 'friend' may be in some danger. Thought I should pass it along, just in case."

Talking to Psychic Junkie didn't exactly quell the anxiety I was beginning to feel about this case. If someone was sending Maggie these dreams, there was little doubt in my mind that the sender was also the killer. Someone who left the letter Z, however subtly, at the scene of the crimes. None of Maggie's clients had a Z in their name, as far as I knew. But, except for Donna Lee, I didn't know their middle names, and for all I knew, Mrs. Bombay was Zelda. I punched in Maggie's number and, as usual, got Buddy instead.

"She's with a client right now. Can I help?"

I couldn't exactly ask Buddy to download the information and send it to me. I was supposed to be a friend and client, not a P.I.

"That's okay, Buddy. How's the head?"

"The stitches already itch, so I guess it's healing just fine. You want me to have her call you back?"

"If you wouldn't mind." Before I could hang up, she went on.

"Hey, we've got a kayak lesson this afternoon, right after her last appointment. Getting ready for the Rogue. You wanna join us? I can teach you easy."

"In the rain? You're going to practice in the rain?"

"Sure. You're not afraid of a little rain, are you? We're going to get all wet anyway. Part of the practice is learning how to flip the boat over and roll right-side-up again. It's called an Eskimo roll and it's a blast. You sure you don't want to learn?"

I didn't tell her I already knew how to do an

Eskimo roll. Maybe not in white water, but I could do one. "I'm sure," I said. "Just tell her I called, okay?" Before Buddy could regale me with any more of her cheerfulness, I hung up, wondering at my sudden bad mood. Jealousy? Or was I just miffed that while I was here trying to figure out who was killing people, Maggie was going to be off playing in the water with Buddy.

Just to prove I wasn't afraid of a little rain, I hopped in my boat and motored to town. I parked at the county dock and jogged all the way to the hardware store where I rented the new release of *The Mask of Zorro*. Then I jogged back, careful to keep the video dry inside my raincoat pocket. By the time I was back home, it had really begun to pour. I fixed myself a cup of hot chocolate and checked my tracking device for the umpteenth time. If Harold was out there roaming around, he hadn't come within five miles of Cedar Hills. It looked like I'd have to make a habit of crawling underneath his truck.

I built up the fire with a few good-sized logs, grabbed the old yellow and blue afghan off the rocking chair and pulled it around me, marveling at how it still smelled of my grandmother's house after all these years, then settled in with my cats to find out what I could about Zorro.

Maggie didn't call me until the next morning and by then I was so miffed I'd forgotten half of what I'd wanted to ask her.

"Late night?" I asked. I'd spent the whole evening cleaning house to the sounds of *Phantom of the Opera* while I tried to ignore the fact that she wasn't calling. I did laundry, vacuumed, dusted, shined mirrors, waxed floors and scrubbed showers, singing at the top of my lungs. By the time I finished, the house sparkled and I felt better. But I was still ticked the next morning.

"Sorry. I did get your message, but I was so exhausted by the time I got home, I just fell into bed. Kayaking's not as easy at it looks. What's up?"

I told her about the Z found etched in Hector Peña's blood and my theory that the killer may indeed picture himself or herself as some kind of avenger, a modern-day Zorro with a twist.

"But I thought Zorro was a good guy. A fun-loving, daredevil type. Not a bloody murderer."

"Think about it, Maggie. This person may *see* himself as the good guy. Avenging wrongs, just like Zorro. Instead of a sword, he used a bat."

"Delusions of grandeur?" she asked.

"Yeah. Picture Zorro with a nasty temper."

"I don't need to," she reminded me. "I was there."

I told her about the tracking device on Harold Bone's truck that so far had yielded nothing. Then I told her about my conversation with Psychic Junkie.

"This is the gay psychic? The weird one?"

"She's not that weird, really. She says that what you're experiencing is telepathy, not clairvoyance. She thinks someone is sending you these dreams. If so, it's probably the killer."

"The killer is sending me the dreams? Can people do that?" She sounded skeptical.

"She says it's pretty rare but not impossible. She also says you may be in danger. Oh. And that feeling you get afterwards? Like you're satisfied? She says that may be how the sender is feeling about having sent you the message. Weird, huh?"

"Creepy is more like it. Have you got any more ideas about who it might be, now that you've met them?"

"It's way too early to tell, Mag. Maybe I'll know more after today's session." I paused, letting my mind work something out. "You know, Martha pointed out that violent crimes are most often committed by men, and it's true. But I've always thought of women as being more psychic than men. If the killer really is sending you these dreams, then we're either dealing with a man who's more psychic than most or a woman more violent than most."

"Man or woman, Cass, I think it's safe to say this person is both more psychic and violent than they want anyone to know."

"So they hide their real identity. Like Zorro behind his mask."

"Maybe," she said. "The Z could mean something else entirely, though."

"Yeah, I know. I don't suppose anyone in your group has a middle name that starts with Z?"

"Just a minute, let me look." When she came back on, she sounded worried. "Joel Zachary Harris," she said. "Damn it!"

"What?"

"I haven't wanted to admit this because I genuinely care for Joel, but of all my clients, he's the one I think is most likely to have psychic abilities. He's very intuitive. Almost painfully empathetic."

"And you didn't think you should mention this?"

"I wanted your objective impression first. I didn't

want to influence your opinion. Besides, I just can't see Joel being that violent."

"They say Bundy was a real nice guy, Maggie. Dahmer was a regular sweetheart. You should have told me."

"I know. You're right. What are you going to do?"

"Find out everything I can about him as fast as possible." I hung up, already planning my next move. The problem was, I couldn't be everywhere at once. How could I monitor all of them at the same time? I didn't really like relying on electronic gadgetry unless I had to, and I already felt guilty about the tracking device under Harold's truck, but what else could I do? Sometimes, part of being a snoop required snooping. Assuring myself that this was a necessary measure, I gathered a few key belongings and headed for my boat.

Joel lived with his mother in one of the older sections of Kings Harbor. The houses were two-story, built in the 1930s when brick was in vogue. Once upon a time, these places had housed the city's elite, but now they seemed more quaint than grand. The front yards still showed a pride of ownership, though, despite the curled wooden shingles on the roofs and the cracked sidewalks. The Harris place was at the end of the block and had a splendid rose garden in front. It was immaculately tended, and already the leaves were turning red, signaling an early bloom. "Thank you, Lord," I murmured, stepping out of the Jeep. I'd been hoping for a way to get my foot in the door.

I was wearing my strawberry blond wig, glasses and lime green jacket, but I was afraid it wasn't enough. Joel had seen me up close, had heard my voice. It was time to whip out the English accent.

Luckily, the mother answered the door. About an inch.

"Yes?" She was a slight woman, with a ramrod spine and steel-gray hair combed back away from her rather prominent forehead. She wore no makeup, and I doubted she ever had. She was much older than I'd expected for Joel's mother. She had the bearing of a Quaker, I thought, breaking into my best British accent.

"I say. I wonder if you could tell me who takes care of these lovely roses out here? I'm putting together a portfolio, you see, of the loveliest roses in Oregon, and I'd very much like to include these, if only I could talk to the tender. I imagine in three weeks or so, these will be quite ready to bloom, and I'd like to have my photographer here, if it's all right. Is the mister in?"

She bristled at this last, although I could tell she'd been taken in by the compliments. "There is no mister to take care of them. I do. Anything you want to know about these roses, you best ask me."

"Ahh, so you're the horticulturist. Why, madam, I am impressed. Have you been at it long? These roses look to be a good forty years old."

"Fifty's more like it. They were here before I bought the place. Been takin' care of them ever since. A few of 'em have died off, here and there, so not all of 'em are that old. I always replaced 'em with the same, though. Those over there are British Queens. You with the newspaper?"

"*Bloom Forever Magazine*," I said, digging out the calling card that identified me as a journalist and

106

hoping she wouldn't wonder why it didn't have more information.

"Never heard of it," she said, peering at me suspiciously.

"We're Canadian, though we're trying to get a foothold here in the lower Northwest. That's why I'm here. What better way to get people interested than in showing them the splendor in their own backyards?"

While we spoke, I kept peering over her shoulder, trying to see into the room. Mrs. Harris didn't miss a thing.

"If you're so interested in the roses, why on earth do you keep looking in here?"

I laughed, thinking the English accent was becoming ridiculous. "Terribly sorry," I said. "To tell the truth, I'm in desperate need of the loo. I was hoping you'd be so kind as to let me borrow yours. I had no idea it would be so far between excellent rose gardens. Our scouts, of course, gave us the addresses, but they didn't say a thing about mileage! I haven't been able to, well, you know, since quite early this morning."

"Rose garden scouts?" she asked incredulously. But to my relief, she opened the door and ushered me toward the bathroom.

The house was both dismal and spotless at the same time. It had the smell of mothballs and something medicinal, a strange combination. I strained my ears, trying to tell if Joel was home, but the only sound came from a radio in the kitchen. No music — just the fevered ramblings of an evangelist.

I shut the bathroom door and leaned against it, wondering if I should go ahead and place the recording transmitter I'd brought behind the toilet, or hope for the chance at a better location and risk not getting to place it at all. The beauty of the transmitter is that it can be concealed almost anywhere and can pick up conversations within a thirty-foot radius. The problem was the same as with my tracking device. Unless I wanted to set up surveillance nearby and monitor the transmitter, I'd have to set it for *Record Only*, then use my cell phone to activate the play-back option. The device could hold up to eight hours of tape and was sound-activated, eliminating wasted recordings. Since all I really wanted was a general idea of what went on in the Harris household, the *Record Only* option would probably be sufficient.

I made a rough estimate of the square footage and floorplan and decided the living room would be a much better spot to place the transmitter than the bathroom. Besides, I didn't really care to hear everything that went on in the bathroom.

I flushed the toilet to mask the sound of the medicine cabinet opening and quickly scanned the contents. From the aftershave, I surmised that this was Joel's bathroom. There was also toothpaste, aspirin, Clearasil, Kaopectate, Tums, Milk of Magnesia, Preparation H and Ben Gay. It seemed little Joel had an impressive list of ailments for such a young man. How many of them were inflicted by the mother? I wondered. Just then, the mother in question knocked on the door.

"Everything okay in there?"

I ran the tap water, closing the medicine cabinet as quietly as possible and told her everything was just fine. Since she wasn't likely to invite me into the living room for a cup of coffee, I'd have to think of something quickly. When I opened the bathroom door, she was standing on the other side waiting for me.

"Uh, this is kind of embarrassing, but you wouldn't have a tampon, or sanitary napkin, would you? It's rather an emergency and I'm afraid I've used my last one."

Her nose wrinkled at the words, but she turned on her heel and marched up the stairs toward her own bathroom. "Haven't needed that nonsense in years, but I may still have a pad somewhere. Wait there."

I'd followed her as far as the living room, and the second she disappeared up the stairs, I rushed for the maple coffee table, practically diving head first in my rush to get the transmitter concealed. Behind me, the sudden bong of a grandfather clock startled me and I banged my head on the table. I was just standing up when she came back into the room, holding the wrapped pad out in front of her like she was carrying a dead mouse by the tail. I grabbed it from her, rushed down the hall to Joel's bathroom and slammed the door behind me.

A few minutes later, knowing I'd already pushed my luck, I thanked the woman for the use of her bathroom, asked her if it was all right to send the photographer by in a few weeks, pretended to make notes on the clipboard I'd brought, then got the hell out of there before Joel came home.

Chapter Eleven

It was almost three when I pulled into Maggie's parking lot and it looked like I was the last to arrive. As nonchalantly as I could, I slipped beneath Harold's truck and clicked on the transmitter's digital read-out. Again, the mileage and direction matched those I'd calculated in my log. It looked like after Tuesday's therapy session, he'd gone straight home and that the rain had kept him from going to work again on Wednesday. Apparently, today he'd gone straight from his home in Riverland to the construction site, to therapy. I reset the device and slid back out, sighing. This was turning out to be a lot of hassle for nothing. I dusted myself off and entered the office.

Buddy was standing at the desk when I came in, apparently afraid to turn her back on the group since being hit on the head. The gauze bandage had been replaced by a tiny, waterproof rectangle and wasn't even noticeable until she turned.

"I heard the kayaking went well," I offered, signing in.

"Dr. Carradine's a natural. She looks good out there, she really does. Like she's been doing it all her life."

I didn't need little Buddy to tell me how good Maggie looked. I turned toward the waiting room.

"You shoulda joined us. I bet you'd look good out there, too. Still water and all."

When I looked back, Buddy was laughing. God, she really did look like Donnie Osmond in his heyday. It was hard to stay mad at her for very long.

"If that was a compliment, thank you."

"Oh, definitely. I mean, it was. I mean . . ." Now she was blushing. This kid could charm the pants off a nun, I thought. I found myself smiling as I entered the waiting room.

To my surprise, Stella Cane was there. My heart skipped when I saw her. I quickly looked away, hoping like hell she wouldn't recognize me. Before I could even sit down, Maggie ushered us all into the group therapy room.

The first thing she did was welcome Stella back and introduce her to me. I was trying to look meek and unassuming and it must've worked because Stella hardly gave me a second glance. Of course, she hadn't heard my voice yet. With any luck, I wouldn't have to do much talking.

"Who would like to start today?" Maggie asked. Everyone was looking at Donna Lee Kramer. Then I noticed the sunglasses and understood.

"You-all want to talk about it?" Mrs. Bombay asked. She was wearing a bright red polyester pants suit that matched her shade of lipstick exactly. Her dyed blond hair had been touched up again, and fewer of the roots showed. Donna Lee shook her head, still looking at her lap.

"Roy again?" Harold Bone asked. His fists were clenched at his sides. Donna Lee nodded and her lip started to tremble.

"What h-h-happened?" Joel asked, eyes wide. His milky skin had erupted in acne since Tuesday. I thought of the Clearasil in his medicine cabinet.

"What happened," Mrs. Bombay cut in, "is that Roy Boy lost his little ol' temper again, didn't he?"

"Please don't call him that," Donna Lee said. "I hate that." She took off her glasses, revealing a purpling bruise beneath her left eye. Stella Cane gasped, then started to cry. "It was my fault this time. It really was. Don't cry, Stella. This isn't like with Hector, okay? We had a fight and I said some pretty nasty things and I, well, he caught me lying to him."

"What'd y'all lie about, darlin'?" Mrs. Bombay asked.

"That's not our business," Maylene said. She was wearing another expensive suit, I noticed. This one was a drab olive green, the color of military camouflage. "She doesn't have to tell us."

"That's okay, Maylene. I . . ." Donna took a deep

112

breath. "He thought I was on the pill but I quit taking them and he found out." Silence filled the room.

"You wanted to get pregnant?" Maggie finally asked.

Donna Lee nodded, starting to cry. "I thought it would make him grow up a little, get more responsibility."

"Bullshit!" Stella's voice startled us all. She stood up, her tear-streaked face red with emotion. "You thought he wouldn't hurt a pregnant woman. Wouldn't hit his own baby!" She blew her nose and mopped at the tears, squaring her shoulders. "I made the same mistake, Donna. And it worked for a little while, too. But not long enough. Pretty soon the baby starts growing, and you can't stay pregnant forever." She was staring at Donna Lee, forcing her to acknowledge the truth in what she said. I was amazed at the change in her. She looked and sounded more like her sister Toby than herself.

"I thought he could change," Donna said. "You're saying they can never change?"

Suddenly, Harold Bone stood up, knocking over his chair. He kicked at it, sending it skidding into the wall. Everyone in the room stayed motionless. His fists were knotted at his sides, the anger so palpable, his eyes bulged.

"Harold?" Maggie said in a soothing voice.

"Goddamn it!" he shouted. The vein near his temple stood out and began to throb. "God fucking damn it!"

Even Mrs. Bombay was speechless. We watched as Harold walked over to retrieve his chair. He picked it up, hefted it over his head and held it aloft. Every

muscle in his body twitched as he struggled with the
need to smash the chair to pieces. Finally, with small,
deliberate steps, he carried the chair back to the circle
and sat down. I realized we'd all been holding our
breaths. No one said a word. Stella, who'd been
standing, slunk back into her own chair.

"I'm sorry," he said. He bowed his head, covering
his face with both hands, and started to sob.

"W-w-what happened?" Joel finally asked. He was
looking from Maggie to Harold and back again,
panic-stricken.

"You want to talk about it, Harold?" Maggie asked,
her voice low and calm. Her eyes were full of empathy
and I marveled at how composed she seemed in the
midst of the maelstrom. Was she accustomed to these
kinds of outbursts? I wondered. Or was she just this
good under pressure?

Harold shook his head but looked up at Maggie.
His eyes were red and swollen. "I'm just so afraid," he
finally mumbled.

"Afraid?"

"That I'll be like him," he said. "My old man.
That I'll take it out on the baby. Bonnie's pregnant. It
scares me to death. What if I lose my temper one day
and hurt him? God, I'd rather die." He started to cry
again, big silent tears rolling down his cheeks and into
his beard.

"Have you ever hurt Bonnie?" Donna Lee asked,
sitting forward in her chair.

"Never!" he exploded. "I'd kill myself first!"

"So what makes you think you'd ever hurt the
baby?" Maggie asked.

He looked down at his fists and started pounding
his thighs. "I lose my temper sometimes. I go out

back and chop wood. Sometimes I want to scream, I've got so much anger. When I'm in my truck alone, sometimes I roll up the windows and howl like a damned animal. It scares me, Dr. Carradine. I can't control my rage. I can't contain it!"

"But Harold" — Maggie's voice was soothing and calm — "it seems to me you are controlling your rage very well. It doesn't hurt anyone to chop the hell out of wood out back, does it? It doesn't hurt anyone to scream at the top of your lungs. The anger you're so afraid of is only dangerous if you don't let it out. It's okay to be angry."

Before he could answer, Stella spoke up. She blew at the blond bangs on her forehead, letting out a mammoth sigh. "Sometimes I wanted to kill Hector. I really did. He made me feel like I was trash. Scum."

The others looked at Stella, clearly surprised at her candor.

Mrs. Bombay started to nod. "I used to dream about killing my mother," she offered. "Sometimes they were night-dreams and sometimes they were just daydreams. I still have them sometimes, even now." The room was silent.

Suddenly, Joel sat forward in his chair. "I-I-I dreamed my m-mother died." Everyone looked at Joel, whose eyes had temporarily lit up. When he noticed the attention, he slouched back in his chair and looked down.

The room was thick with the shared emotion, and everyone seemed to be holding their collective breath, waiting for the next bombshell. Finally Maggie broke the silence.

"I think what we're hearing is that a lot of us have rage and anger, especially toward those who've abused us. Learning to live with that anger is the tricky part, as Harold has pointed out. How can we channel that anger so that it makes us stronger, not meaner?"

She was about to go on when the sound of raised voices filtered through the closed door. Maggie stood up.

"Oh, God. It's Roy," Donna Lee said. Her face was ashen. The voices grew louder and I could hear Buddy clearly.

"You can't go in there!" she shouted. Maggie started for the door. Harold and I were right behind her.

As Roy pushed open the door, Buddy was doing her best to hold him back, tugging at his shirttail, but he was bigger and stronger and dragged her behind him. It was the man I'd seen hosing down the shark blood on the fishing boat next to Donna Lee's houseboat. His dark good looks were ruined by smouldering eyes, and the dark stubble of beard did nothing to hide his clenched jaw.

"Can I help you?" Maggie said, blocking his path. Roy tried to see around her, but Harold and I blocked his view.

"Where is she? You fucking butcher, if you've touched her I'll sue your damn ass to hell and back!"

"I beg your pardon?"

"He thinks this is an abortion clinic," Buddy said, still holding Roy's shirttail.

"A what?" Maggie's voice was incredulous. By now, Roy had seen Harold and me, and a shadow of doubt played at his furrowed brow.

"I know she's in here. Her car's in the lot." He

pushed Maggie aside, stepped into the room and saw the others.

Donna Lee stood, nervously tugging at her long red hair. "What are you doing here, Roy? "

"Are you okay?" he asked, suddenly solicitous. "You haven't gone and done something stupid, after what happened last night?"

"Oh, God, Roy. You thought this was a clinic?"

"Don't try to lie to me, Donna Lee. You know how I feel about that."

"I'm not," she wailed, looking from Roy to Maggie, her face creased with humiliation.

"Listen, dumb shit," Mrs. Bombay said, standing to face Roy. "You thought she was going to get an abortion just because you don't want her to have a baby? Get a life, pal. If and when she ever does get pregnant, she sure as hell won't let some *man* decide whether or not she's going to keep it. For Christ's sake, Roy, grow up!"

Roy looked at Mrs. Bombay with utter confusion. "Who the fuck are you?" He turned to Donna. "What are you doing here?"

"Learning how to say no to assholes who beat her," Harold said, stepping forward. He was about the same height as Roy, but a good fifty pounds heavier, and his fists were clenched in front of him. Donna grabbed him by the arm and I took hold of the other one, just in case.

"And who the fuck are *you*?" Roy asked, sizing Harold up. His voice was full of bravado but Buddy still had him by the shirttail and we pretty much had him surrounded.

"The guy who's gonna teach you a lesson, you ever

lay another hand on her. Anything else you want to know?"

"Hey, I *said* I was sorry. That was between Donna Lee and me. It's no one else's fucking business."

"G-g-go f-f-fuck yourself, mister," Joel stammered, standing behind Maylene.

"Joel, don't!" Donna Lee hissed, real fear in her eyes.

Mrs. Bombay let out a raucous laugh. "That's right, Roy Boy. You think Harold's tough, wait till we sick ol' Joel here on you. You know what's good for you, you'll just high-tail it outta here before we *all* get mad."

By now, Roy was definitely getting antsy. He took a step backward and tripped over Buddy's foot, landing on his rear end.

"You'll be sorry for this," he said, looking back at Donna Lee as he scrambled to his feet. It was all we could do to keep Harold from charging after him down the hall.

That evening, right in the middle of dinner, my high-tech surveillance equipment finally paid off. Harold Bone was on the move. It was just after six when he came within the five-mile radius and my transmitter showed him passing Cedar Hills, heading north on Highway 101. I ran for my boat and gunned it across the lake to the marina, but by the time I reached my Jeep, he was out of range. I headed north and picked him up again halfway to Florence. I stayed back, monitoring his direction and mileage. I had no idea what he was up to. Before he reached Florence, he did a U-turn and headed back south. He never even stopped. I pulled over and waited for him to pass me, trying to see him in the gathering dusk as he sped by. He was bent forward, almost leaning into the steering wheel, but his features were obscured. I turned around and followed at a safe distance, wondering where he was going.

When he reached Kings Harbor, he slowed way down and I had to pull back, letting several cars get between us. He seemed to be cruising now, almost as if he were looking for someone. He turned off into several residential sections, but again, he never stopped. He drove past Martha's condo, and I noticed she wasn't home. He drove past the Harbor Marina where Donna Lee lived on her houseboat and then past Maggie's office, all without stopping. Finally, he pulled back onto the highway and sped up, pushing the green pickup past the limit. I followed him until the turn-off for Riverland and satisfied myself that Harold was finally headed for home. I couldn't help but wonder if he was just letting off steam, driving with the windows rolled up, screaming at the top of his lungs.

By the time I got home my house was dark and cold. I hadn't finished my dinner, so after flipping on the hot tub, I sliced an apple, broke off a chunk of Gorgonzola and poured myself a glass of red wine. Then, throwing a toy mouse down the hall for Panic to chase, I pulled Gammon onto the couch and punched in the number for the transmitter I'd hidden under the Harrises' coffee table. I hit the playback option and waited while it rewound. Even if they were both sitting right there in front of it, I knew they wouldn't be able to hear the tape rewind. The only risk I was taking was if they were saying something important right now.

I stroked Gammon's huge belly and listened to the frantic ravings of the radio evangelist until Mrs. Harris turned the radio off. To my surprise, the recorder picked up the hourly gong of the grandfather clock, making it easy to keep track of the time. It was just after eight when I heard the door creak open and Joel's voice in the hallway.

From the second he came in the door, she was on him, but I could tell Joel was handling things differently than usual. He was barely stuttering, for one thing. And his voice seemed older than it had earlier.

"What do you *mean* you'll think about it? I told you to do it and I mean right now."

"I said I'd think about it, M-Mother. I have a lot on my m-mind right now."

"What has gotten *into* you!" Mrs. Harris sounded furious, but also a little afraid.

"Did I tell you I d-d-dreamed about you last night?" Joel asked.

"What? Don't you get cheeky with me, young man."

"F-f-f . . ."

"What! Spit it out!"

I held my breath, thinking Joel was about to repeat what he'd said to Roy.

"Forget it," he said. The transmitter clearly picked up the sound of the front door slamming.

"Bravo for you, Joel," I said aloud. I fast-forwarded the tape but the only sound came when Mrs. Harris turned on the radio again, so I rewound the tape and reset it to record.

I thought of calling Maggie to tell her of Joel's mini-breakthrough, then thought better of it. She'd looked exhausted after the therapy session, and she still had two clients to go. It was clear this whole mess was taking its toll on her emotionally. The least I could do was let her get some sleep.

I poured myself another glass of Cabernet and went out to the hot tub. The night was clear, and stars studded the sky in a brilliant array of patterns. I slid into the steaming water, careful not to let the bubbles float into my glass, and tried to sort my thoughts. I studied the constellations and listened to a bullfrog singing from the creek, but my mind kept floating back to Maggie. So far, I'd managed to avoid any real conversation with her, but I knew I couldn't put it off forever. I was going to have to come to terms with my own anger. And who was I really angry at? I asked myself. With Maggie for leaving me to care for a dying ex-lover? Or at myself for wanting her back, even after she'd hurt me?

I thought of Donna Lee and Stella, staying with boyfriends who beat them, and shook my head. I'd never do that, I knew. I wasn't about to let someone trample all over me. Is that how I thought of Maggie's actions? Trampling all over me?

"It's something I have to do," she'd said. What choice did I have? Beg her to stay? Insist on going with her? Scream and cry? I'd done nothing. I'd watched her go and it had broken my heart.

I finished the wine and climbed out of the tub, letting the cool night air chill my body. If I was ever going to forgive Maggie, I decided, I'd have to learn to forgive myself first.

"It's okay to be angry," I said aloud to the stars. A

frog croaked in the distance, startling me. "I just need to know if it's okay to still be in love with her?" The frog was far too savvy to answer that one, leaving me to ponder the answer on my own.

Chapter Twelve

As much as I needed sleep, it eluded me, and once again I spent the night tossing and turning. Like a few nights earlier, I felt as if someone were yanking me awake just as I was about to slip into slumber. It was nearly two in the morning when I settled into a half-sleep. Just like before, I seemed to be watching myself dream.

The child was running. Small feet pounded down the wooden stairs toward a triangle of light pouring through the cracked-open door. Almost there! Now, I was the child and I reached out for the knob, my heart surging. The cold metal of the knob was an instant comfort, and I tugged the door open, lunging for safety. But a shadow rose up from behind, looming huge. The door slammed shut and I was yanked back into the room, my arm nearly torn from the socket.

Just before sinking into the black depths of oblivion, I realized that the screaming I heard was coming from my own throat.

I woke with a start, my heart pounding, my throat as raw as if I'd been screaming myself. I clutched the sheets around me, wondering what was going on. Who *was* this kid? Could someone else be in danger? Was someone sending *me* dreams, like they had Maggie? I reached to turn on the light and nearly leaped out of bed when the phone rang. It was still pitch black outside. I glanced at the clock. It was just past two in the morning.

"Cass, I had another one!" Maggie's voice was almost hysterical.

"Are you sure? Maybe it was just a nightmare."

"I don't think so. It was like the others."

"Okay, Maggie. Tell me what happened."

"It's Roy! I just got through hanging him from a giant hook somewhere on a boat!"

My mind raced. "Call Martha," I said. "Right now. Tell her to meet us at Donna Lee's houseboat. I've seen that hook before. It's on Roy's boat and he's tied up in the slip next to Donna Lee's at the marina. I'll meet you there!"

I raced out the door, throwing on jeans, a T-shirt and jacket all the way to my boat. I hurriedly untied the ropes, leaped in and gunned it across the dark, silent lake. It was one of the few times in my life I regretted not having road access.

Once in my Jeep, I put the pedal to the floor and practically flew toward Kings Harbor. There was no one on the road at all. Even the truckers were still sleeping. When I pulled into the Harbor Marina, red and blue lights lit up the place. Martha's Ranger was parked haphazardly next to an ambulance and two patrol cars. Maggie had driven her BMW halfway onto the sidewalk. People had stumbled out of their houseboats and were staring at the commotion. Even the media had arrived, probably picking up the story on their police scanners.

I started toward the *Sea Gypsy* but stopped in my tracks. The paramedics were wheeling a gurney right toward me. Roy's face was beaten to a pulp, and blood soaked through the wrappings around his midsection where a third paramedic was applying pressure. A news cameraman hustled along beside them, filming the scene.

I moved aside to let them pass, wondering if Roy had been conscious enough to tell the police what happened. When I saw Martha, I jogged toward her, but she waved me away. I searched around for Maggie and finally spotted her being questioned by Sergeant Grimes. No wonder Martha didn't want me butting in. Grimes was a self-avowed good ol' boy, an opinionated bigot who thought that women belonged in the kitchen, not on the police force, and certainly not in the private investigating business. I'd learned to steer clear of him as much as possible. I waited back by the cars until Martha finally freed herself long enough to come fill me in.

"The dipshit thinks Maggie had something to do

with this," she said. "The last thing he needs is to see you and her together. It's bad enough that I know her. He's got a real problem with dykes."

"I know, I know. What happened?"

"Someone beat the shit out of this guy, then tried to hang him by the balls. I kid you not, Cass. They put some big old hook up there right through the gonads and pulled him up with the pulley. Luckily for him, his skin tore and he dropped back into the boat. Had he landed in the water, he'd've most likely drowned. As it is, he's barely conscious."

"Did he say who did it?"

She shook her head. "He's not exactly coherent at the moment. Grimes can't believe Maggie dreamed this and that's how she knew. He thinks she's covering for a client. Like someone did the deed then called her, which prompted her to call me, et cetera. Grimes doesn't believe in psychics, Cass. This is going to get sticky, I'm afraid."

"How's Donna Lee?"

"Who?"

"Roy's girlfriend." When she looked blank, I blanched. "You mean no one's even checked? Come on! She lives on the boat next to his." I led Martha around the corner and jogged toward the *Sea Gypsy* which was bathed in light from the commotion on Roy's boat. A local TV station had their cameras trained on the giant fish hook and police were busy trying to keep them from trampling the crime scene. There was no sign of Donna Lee, but her light was on and the door was unlocked. I knocked on the door, then opened it slowly.

"Oh, shit," Martha said behind me, peering into the cabin. I saw Donna at the same time, and my heart lurched. She lay facedown on her bed, her hands and ankles bound behind her. She was gagged and naked. Red welts covered her back and buttocks. She strained to look up, and I saw both shame and terror on her face.

Martha and I moved in unison, untying her as gently as we could. The knots came free with relative ease and I was surprised that she hadn't been able to get free herself.

"What's happening?" Donna Lee wailed when I pulled the gag from her mouth.

"Let me get a clean cloth for your back," I said.

"What's happening!" She pushed the curtain aside and looked frantically out the window.

"Someone beat up Roy pretty bad," I said. I gently pressed a wet cloth to the red welts on her back, wondering what he'd used. From the size and shape, I'd have to guess his belt. Donna Lee pulled away.

"He said he'd hurt me where no one could see this time. To teach me a lesson." Tears had started to fall silently down her face. "God, I hate that bastard."

"Any idea who beat him up?" Martha asked.

"I don't know. He just left me like this. I thought he was coming back. Then I heard all the noise on his boat and I thought he was going to leave for good. I was afraid I'd lie here for days and no one would find me. The next thing I know, there's all these sirens and then you came in and —" She couldn't hold back the sobs any longer. She collapsed onto the bed and let herself cry.

"You better go," Martha said to me. "Wait at Maggie's. I'll need to tell Grimes about this and he'll want to question her. It's going to be a long night."

I hated to leave, but I knew she was right. As

soon as Grimes saw me, he'd be twice as suspicious of Maggie. I slipped out and walked back to my Jeep, blending in with the other lookie-loos as best I could.

It was almost four-thirty before Maggie's BMW pulled into her driveway. I'd been waiting in my Jeep, alternating between dozing off and trying to keep myself awake. The second I saw her, I leaped out and ran to meet her.

"Just hold me," she said.

I opened my arms and Maggie fell against me, wrapping her arms around my waist and pulling me close. She was trembling, and before I knew it, I was stroking her hair, murmuring soothing sounds while I held her. Finally, she pulled away and led me silently to the house.

I followed her through the downstairs office, up the stairs to a place I hadn't been in a very long time: her living quarters.

"It's too early for coffee and too late for wine," she said, taking off her jacket. She walked straight past the kitchen and living room, heading, I knew, for the bedroom.

"Maggie, are you okay?" I asked, following her in the darkness. She hadn't even turned on the lights.

"I'm so exhausted I can't even talk right now, Cass."

I could see her silhouette next to the bed as she peeled off layers of clothing and let them fall to the floor.

"Can I get you something?" Watching her disrobe, I felt an odd lump in my throat.

"You can get your ass over here, slide into this bed and hold me," she said. "I can't seem to stop shaking." She pulled back the covers and slid underneath them, curling into a fetal position.

"Uh, maybe I should get you a blanket..."

"Honest, Cass. I just need to be held."

Dutifully, but with an accelerated pulse, I stripped down to my underwear and shirt and did as she asked.

I inched up against her and wrapped my arm around her waist, careful not to let my hand slide any higher or lower as I pulled her against me. We were touching the entire length of our bodies, and I buried my face in her hair, breathing in the scent I knew so well.

"Thank you," she mumbled into her pillow. Her shivering had given way to a deep, steady breathing, and soon she was asleep. I tried to pull away once, but she stirred, clutched at my hand and held me where I was. The first fingers of dawn lightened the bedroom before I let myself join Maggie in slumber.

Sometime later, the rich scent of her nearness penetrated my sleep and stirred something deep within me. I was suddenly aware that the feel of her satin skin against my body caused me to tremble. Maggie had rolled over and it was no longer her back that pressed against me, but the taut fullness of her breasts.

I thought of pulling away, but when I tried to, she draped a long leg across mine, pinning me beneath her.

"Maggie," I mumbled, but her lips were suddenly brushing mine, silencing my feeble protest, and her hands moved down my body with the sure deftness of someone who knew my body better than I knew it myself.

"I want you," she murmured, her voice full and husky. I felt her fingers and arched to meet them as her gentleness gave way to a pent-up passion that threatened to engulf us both.

Suddenly, I sat up in bed, my heart pounding. The movement caused Maggie to stir beside me, and with a pang I realized that she was deep in slumber, still safely turned away from me. The dream had been so real that my body still trembled with desire. I gazed at Maggie's body, longing to caress her, to pull her to me, to finish what she had started in my dream.

Sighing heavily, I inched back down beneath the sheets, keeping a safe layer of space between us and willed myself back to sleep. Then, for the second time that night, the child took control of my dreams, but there was something terribly wrong.

I was upside down, being hefted by my ankles up toward the barn ceiling. The rope around my ankles dug into the bones and my head pounded with blood. Was the Bad One going to drop me on my head? No. The Bad One was laughing, in a merry mood, and he had tied a bandanna around his eyes and was twirling around in the barn, making himself dizzy. Then I saw the bat and understood. The Bad One was going to play piñata again. I closed my eyes, waiting in terror for the first swing to connect.

I awoke feeling both terrified and angry. That poor abused child was no more than a punching bag, a plaything for an evil, sick monster. But did the child really exist? If so, where? And why was I dreaming about him or her?

That was another thing that baffled me. I could never see the child. I only saw what the child saw and felt what the child felt. Just like Maggie's dreams. Was the person who was sending Maggie dreams also sending dreams to me? But how could that be? I was almost certain Maggie's sender was the killer. And then it hit me. Could this be the killer as a child?

I opened my eyes and realized I was alone in the bed. The smell of coffee wafted in from the kitchen, but the note on the pillow told me Maggie had already gone to work. I looked at her familiar, neat penmanship and smiled at the words.

"I owe you one, sweetpea."

Sweetpea. My cheeks flushed at the memory. Maggie had often called me that after making love, and for a moment, I wondered if somehow, she had been aware of my dream.

I dressed, made up the bed and poured myself a cup of coffee, allowing myself a moment to enjoy being back in Maggie's house. I wandered around, touching the furniture, noticing the changes. There was a new photo on the fireplace mantel and I picked it up, staring into the gaunt, emaciated face of Maggie's ex, Cecily. The chemo had taken her hair but not the light in her fierce eyes. It must've been shot during the remission, I thought. She'd been a beautiful woman, even toward the end. Feeling like an intruder, I carefully set the photo back in its place and went downstairs.

Maggie's office door was shut and I could hear

voices within. I walked out to the front desk but Buddy, who'd obviously already been in, was nowhere in sight. I was eager to talk to Martha to find out what they'd learned about Roy's attacker, so I sat at Buddy's desk and punched in Martha's number. I got her voice mail and left a message, telling her to contact me at Maggie's. There was no one in the waiting room, which I hoped meant that Maggie's nine o'clock appointment would be her last for a while and she could tell me what had happened with Grimes.

Since Buddy had left her computer on, she probably hadn't gone far, I thought. Idly, I clicked on Netscape to check my e-mail and was disappointed to find my mailbox empty. There wasn't even a note from Psychic Junkie. I decided to send her a note myself.

"Hi, P.J. Got another question for you. Is it possible to tap into someone's past? I mean telepathically? For example, could a person who sends one person pictures of what they're doing in the present send another person pictures of what happened to them in the past? Okay, so this is more than one question, but I'm totally confused. Please help."

I was about to sign off when the front door opened and Buddy swept into the room. I hit the send button and stood up, embarrassed to be at her desk.

"Caught you!" she said good-naturedly.

"I was just checking my e-mail," I said, moving around to the other side of the counter so she could sit at her desk.

"Darn, I thought you were finishing my work. Want a doughnut?" She held out the white bag and waited while I chose a chocolate-covered twist.

"You always buy enough for an army?" I asked, my mouth full.

"I saw your Jeep in the lot. I figured you were sleeping in and thought you might be hungry."

I raised an eyebrow and she laughed.

"Maggie told me what happened to our Abortion Clinic Attacker last night. Sounds like he got the crap beat out of him. Though I guess he had it coming."

"Why do you say that?"

"Hey, I'm not dense, you know. Who else gave Donna Lee that shiner? And Mr. Bone was mad enough to tear the guy's head off. I thought we were going to have a real fight on our hands." She ran her fingers through her dark glossy hair and smiled. She was dressed for summer in a white tanktop that showed off her tanned, well-defined biceps, and another pair of plaid shorts.

"So did I," I admitted. "You know what Maggie's schedule looks like for today?"

"She's only got the nine o'clock on Fridays. I was hoping to talk her into some kayaking later this afternoon. Unless you two have plans?" She studied my reaction, clearly dying to know where Maggie and I stood.

"Not yet," I said, returning her frank gaze. Was she just fishing, I wondered, or was she sizing up her competition? Or flirting? Maybe, all three, I decided.

"You wanna see something awesome?" she asked, gracing me with an infectious smile. She held a videotape in her hand. "Come on, I'll show you." I followed her into the waiting room where the TV/VCR unit was mounted to the wall. She slid the videotape into the VCR, pushed fast-forward, then plopped down in one of the easy chairs across from the screen. "This is the training tape I use for swift-water swimming. I could watch it a hundred times. Come on, sit down."

I settled into a chair and watched as the screen filled with rushing, tumbling water. Buddy turned up the volume and the roar filled the room. Then, seeming to remember that Maggie had a client next door, she readjusted the volume.

"Just like being there, isn't it? The guys who taped this were geniuses. They not only had cameramen lining the river on both sides, but they had one in a river raft behind the kayak so you can almost feel the motion. I skipped over the boring introductory part. This is where the guy in the kayak takes what we call a wet exit."

Now I knew why I didn't go for this stuff, I thought. Every now and then the river raft behind the kayak lurched, causing the cameraman to tumble forward, giving the scene enough realism to make me seasick. I watched as the kayak in front bobbed down and shot forward, sometimes disappearing altogether in the treacherous waves.

"This is where you and Maggie are going?" I asked, appalled.

"Oh, no. This is in the class five category. We won't be doing anything more than a class two or three. Okay, watch this!" Buddy was clearly excited. "See that submerged boulder downstream? That's called a strainer. When our kayaker hits it, he's going to go into what we call an Eskimo roll. Normally, he'd pop right back up. The spray-skirt around his waist keeps the kayak watertight, but see how he gets trapped upside down? When that happens, he has to make a wet exit. If he doesn't push himself out and kick free, he's likely to drown. There! Now this is where it gets good. See?"

I watched as the man's head shot out of the water and he took huge gasps of air. The kayak he'd been in had righted itself and was surging ahead of him downstream. Suddenly we were seeing him from a new angle and I realized that a new cameraman had taken over.

"He knows he's in trouble, but he's trying not to panic," Buddy said. "As soon as you panic, your body consumes more oxygen and diminishes your ability to help yourself. Okay, now he's getting oriented. See how he flipped over onto his back with his feet pointing downstream? That's exactly right. That keeps his feet from being trapped by rocks on the river bottom. And as long as he's feetfirst, he has less chance of banging his head around. Even with the helmet, you don't want to meet any boulders head-first." Buddy was standing now, pointing as she spoke. The angle changed as yet another camera picked up the action. "Watch as he gets close to these rapids here. The waves and turbulence make it almost impossible to breathe, so he has to catch a breath in the troughs of the waves, where the water is the calmest. If he doesn't time it right, he'll take in a lungful of water."

"You sound like you've made a few wet exits yourself," I said, amazed at how fast everything was moving. I found myself sitting on the edge of my seat.

Her eyes lit up. "Oh yeah. It's something everyone should practice. Now! See that eddy up there? The calm spot behind that boulder? Our guy here sees that and is heading for it. See how he turns headfirst now? The only time you should ever go headfirst is when you're approaching a strainer like that. It allows you to use your arms to climb over the strainer. In his case, he's going to try to hold himself on that rock. Fat chance."

The rock in question rose a good foot out of the water and was a couple of feet wide. The swimmer headed straight for the rock, using his arms to try and pull himself toward it. Before he could get a strong purchase, the waves behind him carried him right over the rim and flipped him into the eddy behind it.

"Uh-oh," Buddy said. "Here comes the hole."

"Hole?" I asked, wondering how things could get any worse.

"Yeah. It's a place in the river where the level drops way off. The main portion of the current follows the river bottom, but the surface current curls back upstream. If the swimmer gets trapped in it, he'll go 'round and 'round until he's exhausted."

I was exhausted just thinking about it. "There's no way out?" I asked.

"Oh, yeah. There's always a way out. You just gotta know what it is. See how he's going around in circles? He's starting to panic again. Okay, there he goes. He's just figured out he's in a hole and remembers what to do. He's either got to swim to the side or the bottom of the hole and catch the downstream current. Down he goes. In a second, he'll shoot out like a bullet!"

"Am I interrupting a good movie?"

I whirled around and saw Martha standing in the doorway. Her arms were folded across her ample chest in her typical cop stance. She shot Buddy a cursory glance, then did a doubletake. Martha's lesbian radar must've lit up like a Christmas tree because she graced Buddy with a full-on smile. Buddy hit the pause on the remote and beamed back. It was all I could do to stop myself from rolling my eyes.

"Buddy was just reminding me why I prefer calm-water kayaking," I said.

Buddy laughed and started rewinding the tape.

"Girlfriend, we need to talk," Martha said.

I nodded and turned to Buddy. "When Maggie comes out, will you ask her to join us upstairs?"

"Sure thing," she said. "Maybe later I can show you the part where he goes down the falls."

"She's cute," Martha whispered as I led her up the stairs, taking some liberties I hoped Maggie wouldn't mind.

"So I noticed. What's up?"

"You here early or late?" she asked. We walked into Maggie's kitchen and I fixed us each a cup of coffee.

"Late, but it's not what you think. Maggie didn't get home until almost dawn. There was no point in driving back home."

"Uh-huh," she said, sitting at the kitchen table and stretching her long legs out in front of her.

"Martha, tell me what's happening."

"Well, first off, Grimes arrested Harold Bone this morning. The guy with two previous assaults? Seems Donna Lee saw Harold casing the marina yesterday afternoon. And evidently Harold also threatened the guy."

"That's true," I said. "I was there." I told her about the tracking device under Harold's truck and his unusual jaunt up and down the highway.

Martha let out a low whistle. "You saw him go past the marina?"

"Yeah, but he went past a lot of places. He didn't seem particularly interested in the marina. Did you find a Z at the scene by any chance?"

"No. But that doesn't mean it wasn't there. When Maggie called me, two other cops were already on the scene. A neighbor noticed Roy hanging there and called nine-one-one. The paramedics were all over the place. I'm afraid the scene wasn't secured very well. Their first job was to try to make sure the bastard lived. Speaking of whom, I guess he's going to be just fine, if you don't count the impotency problem he's liable to have."

"What did he say about who attacked him?"

"Never saw what hit him. He was in his boat, bending over to get a beer out of the cooler when someone sneaked up behind him and whacked him over the head. That's all he knows."

"And Donna Lee? She doin' okay?"

"She's fine, Cass. Making Harold Bone out to be a hero. I guess it finally got through to her that Roy was bad business. Who needs therapy, huh? All she needed was for someone to beat the hell out of Roy, and suddenly she's a liberated woman. Like she's turned some psychological corner."

"Hmm. It's hard to believe she'd let him beat her like that again. After what happened yesterday, I thought she was going to tell the creep to get lost. "

"You saying you don't believe her?"

"I'm just thinking out loud, Mart. You think someone could tie herself up like that? The knots on her wrists weren't very tight." I took a sip of my coffee.

"I guess it's possible. But she sure as hell couldn't beat herself on the back and butt."

"Okay. But let's say Roy did beat her? Let's say Donna Lee had finally had enough. Picture this. Roy's back on his boat and Donna sneaks up behind him, whacks him on the head with something, then when he's out, she beats the shit out of him. She gets the idea to hook him through the balls and hoists him up on the pulley like a dead fish, then runs like hell back to her boat, stuffs a gag in her mouth, ties her ankles, makes a little loop to slide her wrists through, and just lies there waiting for someone to find Roy."

"And then she hands Harold to us on a platter?" Martha asked. "I can see her getting mad enough to kill Roy, but would she set Harold up like that to take the fall?"

"Maybe she figures there's not enough evidence to convict him. Maybe she just wanted to divert attention away from herself."

"For all we know, someone else may have tied her up," Martha said. "Maybe even Harold. Maybe they're in this together."

The sound of Maggie's footsteps on the stairs preceded her entry. For someone who hadn't had much sleep, she looked pretty good, I thought. She wore a sea-green silk outfit that almost matched her eyes. "Sergeant Grimes still on the warpath?" she asked, coming into the kitchen.

Martha got up to hug her. "He's just arrested

Harold Bone," she said. Maggie's eyes widened and she sat next to me while Martha filled her in on the details, ending with our discussion about Donna Lee.

"I just don't see Harold as being that calculating," Maggie said.

"What about Donna Lee?" I asked.

"I don't know, Cass."

"Well, we better figure it out pretty soon," Martha said. "According to the word in the office this morning, Grimes still thinks you're withholding evidence. He thinks Bone did the deed, then called you up and confessed. In fact, when he finds out about these other murders, he's going to accuse all three of us of withholding evidence. Which, in a way, we are."

"My dreams are my own property, Martha. There's no law that says I have to share them with anyone."

I stood up. "Say that again."

"There's no law —"

"No. Before that. You said your dreams are your property. That's where we've been wrong, Maggie. Remember what Psychic Junkie said? I don't think you're dreaming at all. I think the killer is sending you messages. You think you've just suddenly become clairvoyant? That's not what's happening. You've always been a little telepathic. So have I. The killer is using your ability to receive and is sending you images, but only those he or she wants you to see. Just like the little Zs they're leaving behind. I think the killer is showing off. Whoever it is wants someone to know what they've done." I took a breath. "I haven't told either of you this, but I've started having dreams too." They both listened patiently as I described the dreams. "I think what I'm seeing is the killer as a child."

The room was silent as they let this sink in. Martha stood up and started pacing. Her brow was furrowed. "So now *you're* clairvoyant too?"

"You're not listening, Mart. Not clairvoyant. Telepathic. It's not so much what I can do, as what the killer can do. I'm just receiving the messages. Like Maggie."

Maggie was nodding but Martha still looked skeptical. "Okay, let's get back to something I can make sense of," she said. "Maggie, you said you couldn't see Bone as the calculating type. I agree that our killer is planning these things out. Let's concentrate on that angle. Who in the group *is* the calculating type?"

Maggie shrugged. "The only one who comes to mind is Mrs. Bombay. She once told me that she'd spent an entire year plotting her mother's murder and that the only thing that stopped her from carrying out the plan was her mother's being institutionalized."

"Okay, so maybe she can't kill her mother, but she figures she can help the world out by killing these other creeps," I offered.

"Except these aren't just cold and calculated, Cass," Martha said. "They're also crimes of passion. Whoever's doing it may plan it out, but then they get into it, big-time. You saw the photos of Hector Peña. That was a crime of passion."

"That could be any of them," Maggie said. "Sometimes the ones who seem the most meek are the ones who lose it the most. Someone who's been abused is going to carry around a lot of anger."

"Let's just say it really was a crime of passion," I said. "Maybe Stella, or even her sister Toby, finally snapped and let Hector have it. Maybe the rush of power they felt was so overwhelming, they just had to feel it again. So they thought, why not? It would be easy to push the old Ferguson guy over the cliffs. And then, when Roy made such an ass out of himself yesterday, the old urge kicked in again."

Martha scratched her head. "First you've got someone taking it out on others because they can't take it out on their real abuser and now you've got someone who did take it out on their abuser and liked it so much, they can't stop."

"I hate to muddy the waters," Maggie said. "But it could be a third scenario as well. It could be someone practicing, getting up the nerve to kill the one they really want to."

"Like Joel," I said. They both looked at me and I shared with them what I'd heard between Joel and his mother. "He sounded to me like someone on the verge of something."

"You bugged their house?" Maggie's normally calm voice had risen. "Isn't that illegal?"

"Wiretaps on phone lines are illegal. This is just a little recording device under the coffee table. You said he was the one most likely to be psychic and he *is* the only one with a *Z* in his name. Don't make me feel more guilty than I already do, Maggie. I didn't have a lot of options."

Martha nodded. "I just wish we could eliminate one of them!" she said, sitting back down.

"Maybe we can," I said. "If I'm right and my dreams are of the killer as a child, then it follows that the killer was physically abused as a child. That would rule out the members of the group like Stella and

Donna Lee who are being abused by their boyfriends, right? It would also rule out Maylene. Unless her grandfather beat her in addition to sexually molesting her?" I looked a question at Maggie. When she hesitated, I got mad. "Come on, Maggie. We're way beyond worrying about their damned confidentiality."

She sighed. "Okay, okay. If you're right, then Maylene is about the only one we *can* rule out. As far as I know, the abuse was limited to sexual molestation. But you're making an erroneous assumption about the other two. It's not that uncommon for people who were abused as kids to seek out abusive relationships as adults. Both Stella and her sister Toby were beaten as children. I'm afraid the same is true for Donna Lee."

"Well, we're down to five. That's some progress," Martha said. "But we're running out of time. If Grimes finds out about the other two murders, he's going to be all over Maggie in about two seconds."

"Then we'll just have to beat him to it," I said, more for Maggie's sake than from any real sense of optimism. "There are three of us. If we each take one to concentrate on, maybe we can figure this out. Since Grimes is already working on Harold, we've only got four to worry about."

Martha smiled. "I like that idea, Cass. In fact, I'd be real interested in talking to Donna Lee again. The way she handed Harold to us, and what you said about her maybe faking being tied up like that, it's at least worth looking into."

"I could call Joel and ask him to change his Monday appointment to this afternoon," Maggie said.

"From what Cass overheard and what I saw happen yesterday, it sounds like he really is on the brink of some kind of a breakthrough."

"You meet with him separately, outside of the group?" I asked.

"Yes. That's not uncommon at all."

"Good," I said. "See if you can find out where he went last night, too. Meanwhile, I need to check my transmitter. Maybe I can figure out what time he returned last night and rule him out that way."

"That leaves Stella and Mrs. Bombay," Martha said.

"I'll start with Bombay," I said. "I'm not sure how, but I'll figure out some excuse to run into her in Rocky Point. Stella can wait until tomorrow."

We made plans to reconvene the next day and set out on our separate missions.

Chapter Thirteen

When I went back home to shower and change, Panic and Gammon were beside themselves with neglect. I gave them kitty treats and told them they were the best cats in the world, then I listened to the transmitter I'd planted in the Harris household. Since the recorder was sound-activated, once his mother turned off the radio, the only way I had of knowing how much time passed was the grandfather clock. It was well past midnight when she began ranting and raving and it took me a while to realize she was talking to herself. Or voices in her head, I thought.

I heard what may have been the front door opening and closing sometime past two. Obviously it was after Mrs. Harris had gone to bed because there was no confrontation until morning, when Joel walked right into her trap.

"Where in the hell were you for half the night?" she asked.

"Th-th-thinking," he said.

"D-d-d-drinking is more like it," she mocked him. "Just like your worthless, good-for-nothing father. I ought to wipe that smile right off of your face, you little shit-ass."

"You-you b-b-better not t-t-try it," he said.

"Or w-w-w-what? You going to st-st-stutter me to death?" Her laugh was not just cruel. It was eerie.

"N-n-no."

"N-n-no," she mimicked. "Lord, what a pitiful piece of dung you turned out to be. You know that, Joel? You better apologize right now!"

The tape was silent, making it impossible to know how much time passed. Suddenly, the silence was broken by a high-pitched wail. "Noooo!"

"I said apologize, and I meant it!"

"S-s-s-sorry," he mumbled. The sound of a leather belt cracking against fabric startled me, even from a distance.

"What did you say?"

"I'm s-s-sorry!"

"Okay then. That's all I needed to hear. You want pancakes, sweetie, or scrambled eggs? After all that thinking you must be starving."

I turned off the recorder feeling sick to my stomach. If Joel had been off beating Roy to a pulp, it certainly hadn't done much to fortify him against his beast of a mother.

I apologized to the cats, giving them each an extra treat, and took off for Rocky Point, a sleepy little town, forty miles southeast of Cedar Hills. I hoped it wasn't too late to track down Harriet Bombay. If it was, I'd have to spend the night in my Jeep, something I'd done before but didn't relish.

The drive there was uneventful, save for being slowed down by a road crew that seemed to be doing nothing more than practicing for actual roadwork. The orange cones were out and flaggers enthusiastically waved cars around imaginary obstacles, but for the life of me, I couldn't see any actual work being done. I arrived in Rocky Point around three and located the Bombay residence on the edge of town.

She and her husband lived in a triple-wide mobile home. It was a nice piece of property, with other mobiles scattered about among the myrtle trees and evergreens. It was the sort of place retirees inhabited. I wondered if Mrs. Bombay had married an older man.

After driving past twice, trying to ascertain if they were home, I parked across the street in a clearing about three houses away and watched her house in the rearview mirror. I'd seen someone through the kitchen window but couldn't tell who it was. The station wagon in the carport, however, was the same one I'd seen in Maggie's parking lot, so I was hopeful. Finally, unable to stand it any longer, I dialed their number. She picked it up on the second ring and I immediately hung up.

Now what? I thought. I'd had half a dozen ideas on the way over, but they all depended on when and where I'd see her. For the time being, I'd just have to wait her out, even if it meant spending the night. If a cop came by, I'd have to give it up. Hopefully, none would.

My eyes started to close around six and I was almost asleep when the station wagon backed out into the street. Jerking awake, I threw the Jeep into gear, waited until the wagon was halfway down the street and then turned around to follow. I had no idea if Mrs. Bombay was in the car. I hadn't had time to notice.

The station wagon pulled into a Kentucky Fried Chicken and I followed suit, concocting a plan on the spot. When she climbed out of the wagon alone, I was almost disappointed. I'd wanted to see what kind of man a woman like Mrs. Bombay would marry.

I waited until she was through ordering, then walked inside and studied the array of choices from the menu board on the wall. I was still looking when she wheeled around and practically bowled me over.

"Oh, Lord," she said, stumbling backward, trying to keep her box of chicken from tumbling. She was wearing a bright yellow blouse tucked into blue denim pants with an elastic waistband that had been stretched to the limit.

"My fault," I said, looking embarrassed.

"Well, look who's here. Cassidy, right?"

"Yes. What are you doing here, Mrs. Bombay?" I looked around as if expecting others from the group to materialize.

"Why, I live here, darlin'. What are you doing in little ol' Rocky Point?"

"Just looking, for now. There're a few places for sale around here I might be interested in. I've got it narrowed down to a few towns now. Something small and out of the way." I looked around again. "I need a change of scenery."

"I understand, doll. We all do, sometimes. Say, if you're not in any hurry, why don't you join me for dinner? I can't say much for the ambience, but the chicken's a hell of a lot easier than frying your own."

"Uh, isn't there a rule about not fraternizing outside of group?"

"Oh, hogwash. That's just to discourage romantic entanglements between group members. Trust me, darlin'. You're safe with me." She winked lewdly and I actually blushed.

"Besides, Saturday night's Mr. Bombay's bowling night. I let him out once a week, whether he likes it or not. Gives me a chance to breathe a little. I could use the company." She laughed heartily and headed for a table in the corner while I ordered.

"So, what do you think of our little group?" she asked before I'd even sat down.

"It's weird knowing there are so many others, you know, in similar situations."

"This your first time? In therapy, I mean?"

"In group. I had a therapist before, though. How about you?"

"Ha! I've been shrunk from this side of hell to the other. Psychotherapists, psychologists, psychiatrists, you name it, I've seen 'em. Carradine's not bad, as they go. She handled that hoopla yesterday pretty smooth, I thought. You sure picked a good time to join us. Man, the poop really hit the fan!"

"I'll say. Especially after what happened to that Roy."

"You mean him thinking it was an abortion clinic?

Lord, I damn near peed my pants, laughing over that one."

"No. I mean later. Getting beat up and all."

I watched her reaction. Her painted eyebrows arched and her eyes widened. "Beat up? When was this?"

"Last night. The receptionist told me when I went in today."

"No kidding." She took a healthy bite out of a chicken leg and looked wistfully into space. "I'll be goddamned," she said, her mouth full.

"Yeah. It was just like you told Donna."

"Like what?"

"You told Donna Lee. You said ol' Roy better watch his back or something like that, and sure enough, someone beat him up."

"I did, didn't I? I'll be damned." She started to laugh.

"What?"

"Don't you get it? Someone is out there kicking hell out of the bad guys. I love it!"

"You think so? But how? I mean, who?"

"Well, it ain't me, and you haven't been around long enough for it to be you. I'm pretty sure the doc is clean. So who does that leave?"

"Harold?"

She turned gray eyes to me, studying me closely. "Why him?"

"I don't know. It seemed like he was awfully mad yesterday. And he did threaten Roy."

"So did little Joel," she said. "Sort of. Hell, for that matter, so did I. That doesn't mean anything."

"Well, who do *you* think it was then?"

She chewed thoughtfully, taking a swig of lemonade to wash down the chicken. "That's the problem, darlin'. I don't see any one of them having the balls to do it. I mean, I can see Stella finally offing that turd she was with, and I can see Maylene shoving her granddaddy off the cliff, and hell, I can even see Donna Lee hauling off and beating ol' Roy Boy. But all three of them going off half-cocked? The only thing harder to imagine is any one of them responsible for the whole thing."

The idea that all three attacks might have been perpetrated by different people intrigued me. Could one attack have inspired the next? Could Maylene have gotten the idea after hearing what Stella had done? Could Donna Lee have been inspired by the first two? I shook my head. If so, then who in the hell was sending the "dreams" to Maggie? And to me?

"You ever been psychic?" I asked, my heart thudding. It was a brazen tactic, one that could easily backfire.

"Yeah. Some. I used to sense when Mommy dearest was about to go into one of her episodes. Sometimes, that little inkling would buy me the time to escape. Not often enough, though. Why? You psychic?"

"Lately I've been feeling that way. I've been having dreams. I can't shake the feeling that someone's trying to tell me something. Almost like they're crying out for help."

"That's part of the group thing, doll. You're just being empathetic. You hear all these other problems and pretty soon you start identifying with them. Of course you want to help. That's why group therapy works. We help others where we wouldn't know how to help ourselves."

"You think that's what someone is doing? Helping others in a way they couldn't do for themselves?"

Her eyes narrowed at me and she started clearing her Styrofoam containers. "Your guess is a good as mine, darlin'. Listen, as much as I've enjoyed this little chat, I've gotta skedaddle. Mr. Bombay gets home by seven and he'll have a conniption fit if he finds me gone." She checked her watch. "Damn Sam. He's probably already called out the cavalry." She bustled toward the door and then turned back. "See you Tuesday!"

I waved, watching her go. If she was the killer, she was a good actress, I thought. But then, if she was the killer, she'd have to be.

That night I slept fitfully and woke late, still bothered by the dream I'd just had.

The Bad One was at it again, working himself into one of his fits. He was upstairs, throwing things out of the closet, searching for something. Some favorite torture device, no doubt. I swallowed hard, no longer a child, no longer as afraid. My hands shook, but it was as much from excitement as fear. They were almost adolescent-sized hands, I thought. The nails were bitten to the quick.

The smell of the gasoline permeated the steps as I shook the can, liberally dousing the stairs. I'd wanted to drag something in front of the Bad One's door to block the exit, but I had neither the courage nor time.

If the Bad One came out before the flames took control, it was all over. I fumbled with the matches, cursing my trembling fingers. Finally, one lit and I tossed it onto the steps, watching for a moment in awe as the orange flames licked the steps, gaining momentum as they spread upward. I should have run. My heart was pounding and my legs trembled, but still I stood, watching as the fire burst up the stairs.

The Bad One's door opened and a terrifying shriek pierced the air. I watched, transfixed as the flames engulfed him. His eyes were wild, panic-stricken, looking for a way out. He spotted me and pointed an accusatory finger, the sleeve of his arm already ablaze.

"You!" he shouted.

I smiled, then, the first smile I could remember ever making, and turned toward the front door.

"You're saying the perp killed his or her parents?" Martha asked. It was Saturday morning and the three of us were in Maggie's office, sipping coffee.

"At least one parent. Maybe the father, but from the beginning I haven't been able to tell if the Bad One is male or female. For that matter, I can't be sure about the child, either. The forms seem almost surreal. Of course I've been seeing all this through the eyes of the child, who always seems to see the parent as something more than human."

"Jeez, Cass. It's not that I don't appreciate these psychic dreams, but I wish they'd have a little more detail." Martha grimaced.

"Well, someone is sending us just exactly what they want us to see," Maggie said. "They're manipulating this whole thing. For all we know, that never even happened. Maybe they just want you to think it did."

"Maybe," I agreed. "But let's say it's true. If we knew where each of your clients grew up, we could find out if their house burned down when they were a teenager."

"Why don't we just rule out those whose parents are still living?" Martha suggested.

"But how do we really know?" I said. "Sure, Mrs. Bombay says her mom's in a mental institution, but all we have is her word on that. It should be easy to check, though. Joel's mother is alive, but what about his father? We know Harold's dad is dead but we really don't know how he died. And any one of Maggie's clients could have recreated an identity."

Martha sighed. "Could we put this on hold for a minute and get back to what we found out yesterday?"

I'd been so anxious to tell them about the dream that we hadn't even had a chance to share our findings. I got up and poured us all more coffee. "What happened with Donna Lee?" I asked.

"If she's lying," Martha said, "I sure as hell couldn't trip her up. I questioned her ten different ways and she had the same answers every time. I think she's telling the truth."

"I talked to Joel," Maggie said. "You were right about one thing, Cass. He is on the brink of something. The poor kid is just now figuring out his sexual orientation. He says he spent the evening over in Eugene sitting in the parking lot of a gay bar. Didn't have the courage to go in, but at least he got to see other guys go in and out, and it gave him hope."

"Naturally, no one saw him, right? So there's no

alibi," Martha grumbled. She was clearly growing frustrated with our lack of progress.

"Afraid not. What about Mrs. Bombay?"

I told them about my encounter with the woman and her response to Roy's beating.

"I just don't see all three attacks committed by different perps," Martha said, pushing her brown hair off her forehead.

"I know. Somewhere along the line, I've just assumed it was the same person," I admitted. "Otherwise, how do we explain the dreams?"

"So, we're back where we started," Martha said. "And now it looks like we can officially add Maynard Ferguson to the list, too. The autopsy report ruled out heart failure. Either the old man wheeled himself off that cliff, or someone pushed him. Either way, it was the fall that killed him, not his heart. He was alive when he hit the rocks."

"I knew it," Maggie said, shaking her head.

Martha went on. "Meanwhile, Grimes is perfectly content to hang Roy's attack on Bone. The fact that he verbally threatened to harm the guy in front of eight people doesn't help. And Donna Lee *did* see him driving by her place that afternoon. Mrs. Bone swears Harold was home all night, but what wife wouldn't? I'm surprised Grimes hasn't started questioning the other group members yet."

"He tried," Maggie said. "Right after you two left yesterday, I went out for a while. When I got back, Grimes and Officer Dale were here waiting for me."

"Oh shit," Martha mumbled.

"That's what I thought. Buddy was handling them pretty well, though. They kept trying to sweet-talk her into giving them last names, but she held them off until I got here. I was afraid she'd mention the missing file and the fact that someone had conked her on the head to get it, but she came through like a trooper."

"What did you do?"

"I read them the riot act on confidentiality and asked them to leave. Grimes said he could get a warrant, and he and I went head to head for a while. I was starting to think I'd won, but the way he was smiling when they left made me feel like it wasn't over yet."

"Where did this conversation take place?" Martha asked.

"In here. Why?"

"And were both men with you the whole time?"

"Yes. Why?"

"How about before you arrived? Did they ever leave Buddy's sight?"

"I don't know, Martha. Why are you asking me this?"

"Because I know Grimes. Wait here." Martha walked out to the reception desk and when she returned a few moments later, her face was flushed. She grabbed a pen off of Maggie's desk and scribbled on a piece of paper. Then she held it up for us to see the words: *We're fucked!*

"What?" Maggie asked.

Martha held her finger to her lips and scribbled again: *Bugs!*

Maggie furrowed her brow but I was already on my feet. I grabbed the pen from Martha and wrote my own question: *Where?*

She shrugged and wrote hurriedly. *Buddy says Officer Dale asked to use the restroom. He could've ducked in here or into the group therapy room. Come on, let's check.*

We started with her office, working our way silently around the room, looking under chairs, crawling beneath her desk, searching inside lampshades, beneath her sculptures and behind the pictures on her walls. Martha was taking the phone receiver apart when I clapped my hands. She and Maggie looked up sharply and I pointed to the bottom of an earthenware flower vase in the corner, lifting it up for the two of them to see.

"Son-of-a-bitch!" Martha mouthed, motioning us to join her in the hallway. "I knew he'd do something like this! The man has no scruples. What a scumbag."

I didn't want to remind her that I'd recently employed a similar device myself.

"Why would he bug my office?" Maggie whispered, even though we were in the hallway.

"Because Grimes thinks Harold confessed to you and he's probably hoping that he'll tell all in your next session. If he does, Grimes can get it all down on tape."

"But it would be inadmissible," Maggie said. "Wouldn't it?"

Martha shrugged. "Grimes would figure out a way to use it, Mag. Come on. We better check the group therapy room."

This time the job was far easier, because there were fewer objects to search. I started with the paintings on the wall while Martha began rolling back the Persian carpet in the center of the room, then checking underneath the chairs in the circle. It was behind the fifth picture that I found the tiny device. Before I could even get her attention, Martha was waving me over excitedly. I pointed to the bug and her eyes grew wide. Then she tipped over the chair that Maggie usually sat in and it was my turn to look shocked.

"Two?" I mouthed, holding up my fingers. We examined the two devices side by side. Mine matched the one found in Maggie's office, but the other one was a different model, size and shape. Quickly and silently, we resumed our search, overturning every stick of furniture and object we could find until we were satisfied there weren't any others.

Martha motioned us out into the hallway, past the waiting room to the front door. None of us spoke until we were well outside.

"I don't get it," Maggie said. "Two bugs in the therapy room?"

Martha frowned. "Exactly. It doesn't make sense. One bug is more than ample to project anything said in there, even in a whisper. With your office and group therapy room covered, there was no need for the third device."

"Then why?" Maggie looked miserable.

"Someone else," I said.

Maggie looked at me oddly. "Not you?"

"Oh, come on. Of course not me. Someone who wants to be privy to what's said in your sessions."

"Damn!" Martha muttered. "Here we've been concentrating on ruling group members out, when we should have been opening it up!"

The three of us stood in the parking lot, staring at one another.

"Like who?" Maggie finally asked.

"What about Buddy?" I asked.

Maggie frowned, shaking her head. "I don't think so. It doesn't make any sense. Besides, what about the missing file? Someone hit her on the head to get it."

"What about that Toby Cane?" Martha asked.

I had no trouble picturing big Toby sneaking up behind Buddy to steal the file. In fact, I could easily imagine her hoisting Roy up on the hook. I nodded. "You know, I've thought it was possible that Stella was telling Toby what went on in therapy. That maybe Toby has this Zorro complex and she uses the information to fulfill her needs, or whatever they are. But maybe Stella wouldn't tell her anymore, and Toby decided to take matters into her own hands."

"Can just anyone get into your group therapy room, Mag?" Martha asked.

She sighed. "I wouldn't think so. But when I'm with a client, the front door is unlocked. People in the waiting room would have access, I guess. Buddy checks everyone in, though."

"Sure," I said. "Like she checked in Roy and Sergeant Grimes. And the other day, when I came downstairs, Buddy wasn't even here. She'd gone for doughnuts."

"So much for security," Martha said.

Maggie shook her head.

"Hey," I said. "This isn't necessarily a bad thing. We were running into brick walls before. Maybe now that we have a new perspective, things will fall into place."

"Not to be the bearer of bad news," Martha countered, "but Grimes just heard everything we said in Maggie's office. Or he will, just as soon as he listens to his tape. For all we know, he's sitting one block over, listening right now. I have a feeling the three of us are going to be feeling some serious heat and soon."

"He's going to be coming for me, isn't he?" Maggie asked. "I've got to hide my records. If I have to, I'll tell him about the dreams, but I've got to protect my clients." She started to pull away.

"It's Martha we should be worried about," I said. "The second Grimes hears that she's been privy to this information, he's going to come after her with both guns blazing. I think we need to do a little damage control."

"I'm afraid it's too late for that," Martha said.

"Not necessarily. Grimes doesn't know we found the bugs." I shrugged.

Her eyes lit up with understanding and Maggie nodded. "You think we should go back in there and fake a conversation?"

"I do. I think we should stage a scene where Martha says that even though she doesn't believe in all this dream hogwash, she's going to tell Grimes what we've told her, on the off-chance that there's anything to it. You can beg her not to tell, Maggie, but she'll make a big show of being bound by duty, et cetera. Then she can put in a call to Grimes when she knows he's out, ask him to page her, and then claim her pager wasn't working. It'll buy us some time."

"Grimes is almost dumb enough to fall for it," Martha said. "I think we should do it."

We started to walk back across the lot.

"Wait," Maggie said. "If Grimes doesn't know we found the bugs, neither does whoever put the other one there, right? And we're assuming that's the killer."

160

"Right," Martha and I said in unison.

"So, why can't we stage another conversation?"

"You mean, lay a trap?" Martha asked.

I was already nodding my head. I liked the idea. "It might work, Maggie. After Martha leaves, you and I can have a therapy session. I'll divulge the truth about my abuser. Maybe I can get someone to pose as my boyfriend, or . . ."

"They already know we're friends if they've been listening in, Cass. In fact, they probably already know a lot more about you than you think. If they're going to buy the therapy session, then we've got to make it real."

"How do you mean?" I asked, starting to feel uneasy.

"You've been emotionally abused, Cass. By me. That's the only way this thing will fly. I'll play the part of the cold-hearted, detached therapist. Whoever's listening will have no doubt that I'm a heartless bitch. Meanwhile, you play the part of the giving, loving victim, too hurt to stand up for yourself."

"No way anyone's going to believe that I'm a victim, let alone that you're a heartless —"

"Bitch, Cass. Yes they will. We'll convince them. You've played roles before. We can do this." Maggie was looking at me with determination but I was shaking my head.

"I don't like this Maggie. Any of it."

"They'll come after you," Martha said to Maggie. "That's what you're suggesting, right?"

Maggie nodded. "It stands a chance of working, Martha. You can set up surveillance outside, can't you? See who comes to get me? I mean, if we do this right, we can have them walk right into the trap."

"Maggie, this is a dumb idea," I said. "First of all, the killer identifies with you, or else they wouldn't be sending you the 'dreams.' You really think they'd come after you?"

"They obviously identify with you, too. That they thought they could trust me makes this even better. It will be the ultimate betrayal. What could be worse? A therapist who counsels the abused turns out to be an abuser herself! It could send them right over the edge."

"It could work," Martha said. "You really think you could pull it off, though?" She looked skeptical.

"No one will believe it, Mag." I said. "You're —" I paused, trying to think of the right phrase. "You're too nice."

"Watch me," she said, folding her arms across her chest. We stood in the parking lot, silently staring each other down. Maggie finally broke the silence. "Look. If this doesn't work, then I'll cooperate with Grimes and tell him everything. But right now, he's willing to hang Roy's beating on Harold and I don't know if he's right. This is something we've got to try, Cass. We're not going to get another chance."

"Can we assure her protection?" I asked Martha.

"We can take turns watching the place. I'd feel better if we could hide Maggie at night, though."

"Things have to appear normal," Maggie argued. "You two can work out the surveillance details later, but I'm staying in my own home. Come on, let's get started." She took me by the hand and squeezed gently. "Let's give them the performance of a lifetime."

Chapter Fourteen

Martha had missed her calling. By the time she was through delivering her "bound by duty" speech, I was almost convinced myself. Before she made her grand exit from the group therapy room and left Maggie and me to fend for ourselves, she flashed me a note. *Meet me at Pepe's when you're done.*

I nodded and turned back to Maggie, who said, "As long as I have you here, Cass, there are some things I think we need to discuss."

And so the scam began. I wasn't sure how it would play out, but my heart was racing. Maggie, ever the skillful therapist, prodded me gently, pulling my feelings to the surface until, before I knew it, I was talking freely.

"You feel that I deserted you?" she asked.

"You did, Maggie. It's not that I feel you did. You did."

"Semantics, Cassidy. My point is, you feel wronged. That's so typical."

"What do you mean? Typical of what?"

"The weak always feel wronged. Instead of doing something about their problems, they just whine about them. That's what you're doing now. You're whining."

She was laying it on a bit thick, I thought, but she was on a roll.

"You're weak, aren't you Cass? Isn't that what this is really about?"

Despite myself, I was getting mad. "If 'weak' means letting yourself be hurt, yes, I guess I am. If 'weak' means loving someone even after they've hurt you, yes. But if strong means you can walk all over someone and not even feel bad, then I guess I'd rather be weak."

Maggie laughed. It was so unlike her, so atypically cruel, that despite the fact that I knew she was acting, a chill ran through me. "You know what's so pathetic, Cass? You can't even bring yourself to get mad. Part of you hates me for what I did, but you'd take me back in a second. If I walked over there right now and kissed you, you'd let me. Wouldn't you?"

I was suddenly panic-stricken. "I — I don't know."

"Yes, you do. Even now, just thinking about it excites you. You want me, Cass. You hate me and you want me. Which is precisely why you need a therapist."

"This was a bad idea, Maggie. I should never have agreed to see you in therapy."

"Too late for escape, sweetheart. We're here, so we might as well work it out. You've got to make up your mind. Hate me or love me? Which is it going to be?"

"Maggie, don't."

She was on her feet, moving slowly toward me. "I'm going to kiss you, Cass. And you're not going to resist at all."

"I don't want that."

"Prove it," she said. "Fight me."

"Don't," I said, albeit weakly. Maggie was standing right in front of me, inches away. I knew she was only acting, but my throat was tight and my voice wavered. "Please, Maggie."

We stood for an eternity, our gazes locked in combat that wasn't entirely feigned. Finally Maggie touched her fingers to her lips, then pressed the same fingers to my lips, mouthing a silent apology. Then she slapped me.

"What the hell?" I said, stumbling backward.

"You see!" she said, her eyes almost brimming with tears. "I can kiss you any time I want. I can slap you any time I want. You are weak, Cassidy James. Which is fine. I like women that way. But let's not get any more ideas about complaining, shall we? As long as you know who's boss, we'll be just fine. Am I right?"

I was staring at her dumbly, still holding the cheek she'd slapped. Maggie was pushing this acting thing to the limit.

"I asked you a question, Cass. Am I right?"

"Yes," I muttered.

"Fine, then," she said, returning to her desk where she started scribbling on a piece of paper. "I've got a

165

busy weekend, but I think I should see you before Tuesday. You know, I do expect you to participate this time. You need to acknowledge your weakness, Cassidy. Show the others who you really are. It makes them feel good to see other weak, clinging, pathetic creatures. Especially the way you come off as so tough and competent in public. They need to see the coward beneath the surface."

"I'm not a coward, Maggie. It's just with you. You know I'd do anything for you. Why do you want to hurt me?"

"Because I can, babe. Because you let me."

"And if I didn't let you, would you still want to, you know, see me?"

She laughed. "We'll talk about that later. Time's up. How about, say, Sunday morning? Nine o'clock?" She was making Martha look like an amateur, I thought.

"Tomorrow?" I asked meekly.

"Yes, tomorrow. You have a problem with that?"

"No, Maggie. Tomorrow will be fine."

She held up the paper so I could read her writing. *I will make this up to you, I promise!* it said.

I grabbed the pen off her desk and scribbled back. *I just hope you haven't gone too far!!!*

I'm afraid I may have let the door bang behind me.

"Everything okay?" Buddy asked when she saw me headed for the door.

No, I wanted to tell her. *Everything is not okay.* But I returned her smile and nodded, letting myself out.

* * * * *

Pepe's was in full swing, and Martha, off-duty, was sipping the remains of a margarita. "Well, how'd it go?" she asked, signaling the waitress for two more.

"I feel sick," I admitted. "She slapped me."

"What?"

I described our interaction and Martha laughed. "Too close to the truth for comfort, eh?"

"It was awful, Mart. I knew she was acting. I could tell by her eyes that it was killing her to say those things, but still, I couldn't help feeling like she really was talking to me. Am I weak?"

Martha threw back her head and laughed. "You're kidding, right? I'll admit you're a pushover when it comes to women, but you're not weak. Not when it counts. Maggie knows that, babe. She knows she hurt you, and I don't mean today, but she doesn't think for one second that you're weak. Cheers." We clinked glasses and I let the icy tang of the lime and tequila trickle down my throat. "You think the perp will bite?" she asked.

"Well, Maggie was pretty convincing, but it might take more than this. We set up another 'session' for tomorrow morning. You tried calling Grimes yet?"

"Ten minutes ago. As usual, he was already out to lunch. This was the one place I knew we'd be safe. The guy hates Mexican food. I left a message for him to call my pager. You want the number seven?"

The waitress took our orders and Martha filled me in on her plan.

"I'm liking the sound of that Toby Cane better and better," she said. "I'm going to see if I can pin her down on an alibi for the night Roy got beat up."

"Sure," I said. "Stella will say they were at home together watching TV."

"Maybe Stella doesn't know what Toby's doing," Martha mused. "Maybe I should talk with her first."

I nodded. "I'd definitely start with Stella and work my way up to Toby. Just don't catch her in a bad mood. The woman has got a temper."

"So does the killer, Cass. That's one reason I want to talk to her."

I scooped salsa onto a corn tortilla chip and ate it. "If it is Toby, and you scare her away, the trap we just set with Maggie won't work."

"Well, if Maggie was as convincing as you say, maybe she'll strike tonight."

"Somehow, I don't think it'll happen that fast," I said.

"You're probably right. But if nothing happens tonight, I'll drive to Eugene tomorrow anyway. By Monday morning, I'm going to have to bite the bullet and face Grimes." She took a sip of her margarita and leaned back. "You know that idea about trying to find out if one of the clients' parents burned to death? I know a guy who might be able to make that go a lot faster for you. If you can get hold of him. He's a computer geek who does research for the department sometimes. Free-lances for spare change, but his real love is hacking. If the info you need is on a computer somewhere, he's the one to find it. Guy's name is Todd Pal. If you tell him I sent you, he'll help you out. Tina defended his brother on a misdemeanor last month."

I doubted there'd be much computerized information about decades-old arsons, but it couldn't hurt to check it out. I wrote down the name and number and then concentrated on my food while Martha and I worked out our surveillance schedule. We decided that

168

I'd take the first shift, watching Maggie's place from dusk until midnight. Martha would relieve me from midnight until about eight Sunday morning, when I'd take over again so she could go talk to Toby Cane in Eugene.

I pushed back my chair and reached for my wallet, but Martha waved me away. "This one's on me, babe. Go find out what you can about house fires."

Todd Pal was pencil-thin, with fine black hair combed straight back and a scraggly goatee that didn't do a thing to make him look older. I put him in his mid-twenties but he could easily pass for eighteen. He wore a half-dozen earrings in his right ear, another in his nostril, and no doubt a handful of others in places I didn't care to imagine.

"Martha Harper?"

"The cop. Tina's friend. The one who defended your brother?" We were sitting in his downtown apartment in what must have been a living room at one time. Todd Pal had converted it into a computer center, and screens glowed benevolently from gray and silver boxes everywhere I looked. The room hummed with electricity.

"Oh, yeah. *That* Martha Harper. Sure I know her. Good people. What do you need, exactly?"

When I told him, he laughed. "This could take for-fucking-ever. If I had some names to start with, it would sure help." He was already moving toward a large monitor whose screen saver flashed multi-colored geometrical designs.

I deliberated giving him the list of Maggie's clients.

With the names, he could probably do this in a few hours. Without them, he'd be operating in the dark. But Maggie would never forgive me. I shook my head.

"How about a range of dates, then?" he asked, his fingers dancing across the keyboard. "Something to narrow this down." He looked at me hopefully.

I'd already worked out the range by taking the oldest group member, Mrs. Bombay, and subracting thirty-five years, which would put her at about the right age for the teenager in my dream. Joel would have been that age about seven years ago. I told him and he laughed again.

"Nineteen sixty-three through nineteen ninety-one? You're kidding, right?"

"You can't do it?" I'd figured it was a long shot.

"I didn't say that," he said, pulling at his earlobe. "What else you got to go on?"

"The fire was deliberately set with gasoline, I think. There might be mention of a child missing. Around fifteen years old."

"Is the burn vic male or female?" he asked, already punching keys on his computer.

"I'm not sure."

He rolled his eyes, but kept working. "And this could be anywhere in the U.S.?" If he was trying to make me feel bad, he was succeeding. "There's going to be a whole lot of these. We need descriptors. Isolators. Connectors. Something we can cross-reference. Something to narrow down the search."

"There might have been a letter Z involved," I said.

"What do you mean?"

"I'm not sure. Maybe the victim's last name began

with a *Z*." This was no more far-fetched than my Zorro theory, I thought. "Maybe the police mentioned finding the letter *Z* near the scene. It's a long shot."

"Lady, this whole thing is a long shot. What else?"

"The person who died in the fire may have been an abusive parent. There could be a record from child protective services, but the records would be sealed."

"No such thing as a sealed record," he said, grinning. "And that's exactly the kind of stuff we need. What else?"

I thought, racking my brain. "It's a two-story house," I said. "And there's a barn."

He shot me an odd look, then punched in some more keys. "Okay. Rural. That's good. Not too many barns in big cities. Keep going."

I thought back through the dreams, remembering the first one. Something about a kitten. "There's a creek!" I nearly shouted. "Somewhere close by, there's a creek." The creek where the monster had drowned the kittens.

"Good. That rules out deserts, anyway. See? You knew more than you thought you did. Anything else?"

I racked my brain, forcing myself back into the murky dreams, letting myself feel the terror as I revisited the horrid events of the killer's childhood. Todd had stopped working and was watching me, one dark eyebrow raised expectantly.

"Mothballs!" I said. "The place reeked of mothballs and mildew. The house was old and damp."

"Okay?" Todd was obviously waiting for more.

"The person drank a lot, too."

"Think they went to AA?"

"I doubt it." I shook my head, trying to think.

There was something I was missing. It was in the last dream. I closed my eyes, willing myself to go back into the house.

The child had poured the gasoline on the stairs and was watching the flames shoot up the stairway. The door opened. The Bad One was standing in the doorway, pointing down, even as the flames engulfed his body. And right there, over the Bad One's shoulder, hanging on the opposite wall was a hatrack. And on the hatrack was a uniform.

"Military!" I practically shouted. "I think they were in the military!" I closed my eyes again and described the uniform as well as I could.

"Sounds like the army," Todd said. "I'll double-check. This could help a lot. Even if the uniform belonged to a spouse, it will help. Anything else?"

I knew I'd exhausted my limited knowledge and shook my head.

"Okay, then. Let me see what I can do. It's going to take a while, you understand. And I'm not all that optimistic. The best I'll be able to get you is a list of possibles, and the list will be long. If you want, I can download it and e-mail you when I've got it."

"That would be great," I said. "How much do I owe you?"

"I'll let you know when I see how long this takes me. Don't worry. I'm not cheap, but I'm fast and honest."

I left him my home phone number and e-mail address, sending a silent prayer skyward as I walked out.

* * * * *

Todd Pal had warned me, but I still wasn't prepared for the sheer volume of data that he sent me. I'd spent the afternoon doing errands and was just getting ready to leave for my first watch of Maggie's place when the e-mail came in. There was no way I'd have time to print it all out. I decided to take my laptop with me.

I apologized to the cats for leaving them again so soon, then made my escape before Panic could dash out the door between my feet.

The evening sky was clear and already studded with stars when I pulled up to the curb across the street from Maggie's. I parallel-parked between a red van and a green Ford Escort, which pretty much concealed my position from either direction while affording me a straight shot of Maggie's front door and parking lot. The tiny lot was empty, and the light coming from Maggie's upstairs living room window indicated that she was home. I pushed the front seat back as far as it would go, connected my laptop to the wireless modem, making sure my back-up batteries were handy, then settled in for some tedious, eye-straining work. My thirty-eight was tucked safely in my shoulder holster, just in case.

Todd had organized the data by ranking the percentage of matching fields, which he explained in his brief salutation. Each "episode," as he called them, was numbered in descending order by its corresponding percentage score. A perfect score would indicate that the person who'd died in the fire had a first or last name starting with Z, had been in the Army, was on file as a child-beater, lived in an old two-story house with a barn in a rural community with a creek nearby. My heart skipped as I stared at the only episode meriting a perfect score. I clicked on the More Info box and waited for the original clipping to come on screen. It was dated March, 1970, and came from Little Rock, Arkansas, where a Ziggy Jones had died from what appeared to be an intentionally set fire to his two-story farmhouse. Authorities had not ruled out the possibility that the arson and resulting murder were racially motivated. My moment of optimism faded as I realized Ziggy Jones was black.

I continued to glance out the window toward Maggie's front door as I worked my way down the list, jumping from the one perfect score to the dozens upon dozens of those in the tenth percentile. Apparently, it was far more common than I thought for people to burn to death in their own homes. It seemed especially common in rural settings, where people lived too far away from fire departments and neighbors who might notice the smoke. To top it off, quite often the cause of the fire was a tipped-over kerosene lamp, making it difficult for authorities to rule out arson. I closed my eyes, wondering how on earth I was going to find the right one, and wondering if it was even on the list.

I looked out at Maggie's window, wondering what she was doing. She wasn't much of a TV-watcher, I knew. Probably reading a book, I thought. I wished I could call her, but Martha and I had already decided against that unless, of course, it was to warn her that there was trouble. We were afraid that someone, either Grimes or the killer, might have somehow tapped her phone, and we didn't want to take any chances.

I looked back at my screen and continued to scroll down the list. Maybe I should be looking for the least-common field, I thought. If they weren't locked, I could try to list the cases by specific fields, such as *Child Abuser*, and just bring those up. But after wasting an hour, I realized that the way Todd had set up the data, I didn't have that option. Using my cell phone, I punched in his number and waited. I left a message on his answering machine, telling him my problem, and asked him to please call me back if he got in before midnight. Then I continued to scroll through the cases, hoping that something would jump out at me.

When my e-mail box chirped at me, I nearly bolted off the front seat. "Thank God," I muttered, thinking Todd was getting back to me. Instead, I had a message from Psychic Junkie.

"Hello there, stranger. Sorry I couldn't get back to you sooner. Things have been hectic here. To answer your question, there's no reason a good sender couldn't be sending you memories just as easily as their present thoughts. But beware, someone this gifted could also be sending lies. Is this person manipulating you? Be careful, my friend. I sense that danger is near."

Terrific, I thought. This whole arson thing could be a deliberate attempt to lead me down a false path. I closed my eyes and tried to imagine how the killer had felt back then. "Who are you?" I asked silently. "And what do you want from me?" I listened as hard as I could, willing myself to open up to whatever vibes the killer could send me. My phone rang, making me start for the second time.

"Todd?"

"Sorry. It's just me," Martha said. "Anything happening?"

"Nothing. All is quiet." I glanced up at Maggie's window and realized she'd turned off her lights. When had that happened? "Sleeping Beauty is all tucked in," I told Martha.

"I'm on my way. When you see my lights, pull out and I'll take your spot."

"It can't be midnight already," I said, checking my watch. To my surprise it was quarter till.

"Time flies when you're having fun, babe. Go home and get some sleep. We'll swap stories in the morning."

I barely had time to shut down my computer and adjust my seat before I saw Martha's headlights in my rearview mirror. I pulled out onto the empty road and yawned the entire drive back to the marina.

Chapter Fifteen

Sunday morning, the sun blazed through my window even before my alarm went off. I hurried through my shower routine and dressed as quickly as I could, trying to appease the cats who were incredulous that I was taking off again so soon.

"We'll have fresh fish tonight," I promised, racing out the door. I hopped in my boat and gunned it over to the marina so I could relieve Martha on time. I'd brought my laptop and recharged batteries with me, hoping to put in another hour before my appointment with Maggie. On the way, I stopped at a Gas Mart and bought two large coffees and a couple of packages of miniature doughnuts.

"Sustenance," I said, opening the passenger door of Martha's Blazer.

"Jesus Christ, Cass. I didn't hear you come up."

"That's 'cause you were sleeping," I said, grinning.

"I was not."

"You were too. I could hear you snoring a block away."

She reached over and slugged me in the arm, almost making me spill the coffee. I handed her one of the Styrofoam cups and slid into the passenger seat. "I take it all is quiet on the western front?"

"Quiet as a titmouse. Whatever that is. It does stir the imagination, though. You get any sleep?" She reached over and helped herself to a package of doughnuts.

"Some," I admitted. "I'm sort of dreading my nine o'clock appointment. I was kind of hoping someone would approach last night, just to get this over with."

"Me too, babe. Listen, if something happens, don't go playing hero, okay? Call nine-one-one, then call Grimes, in that order."

"Don't worry, Martha. I can take care of myself. You sure you're up for driving to Eugene? Maybe you should get some sleep first."

"Nah, I'm good to go, as they say. A little caffeine and sugar, and I'm primed. I'll call you when I get back in town."

I climbed out of the Blazer and watched her pull out and make a U-turn. Then I walked back to my Jeep and waited for nine o'clock.

By eight fifty-five, no one had shown up and I was bored. I locked the Jeep and crossed the street, letting myself into Maggie's office. She was waiting for me by the front door, fully outfitted in her kayaking garb.

"You expecting a flood?" I asked, trying to sound light-hearted.

"This is the big day," she said. "Buddy and I are going to shoot the rapids. That's why I wanted to meet you early. Come on, we should get started."

"Wait a second," I whispered, pulling her back. I wasn't entirely sure our voices weren't being picked up. "You think that's a good idea, in light of what's happening?"

"The rapids? Hell, Cass. They're not going to be any more dangerous today than they will be a week from now. Besides, given the circumstances, I'll probably be safer there than here." She had a point, I supposed. And it would mean I didn't have to spend the day parked across the street watching her house. I followed her into the group therapy room and sat down.

Maggie looked at me questioningly, obviously expecting me to start the charade.

"I've been thinking it over, Maggie. I don't think it's going to work, seeing you both professionally and, you know, personally."

"Fine, then. Let's cool the relationship until your therapy is completed."

"That's not what I meant," I stammered.

"Of course not. You'd rather take the easy way out and quit therapy. Right?"

"I could see someone else. Someone more objective, maybe."

She let out a harsh, cruel bark of laughter that made me start. "Ha! You want another therapist, is that it? Someone who will coddle you, placate you, make you *feel* better? For God's sake, Cassidy. You are pathetic!"

"I don't see why it's such a bad idea." I put a whine in my voice that made me cringe. I didn't like this role at all.

"I'll tell you why. Another therapist won't know you the way I do. They'll spend months, maybe years, working on all the wrong things. Not that you don't have plenty of things to work on. But they'd never get down to the real problems. They'd get all hung up on the relationship thing."

"What relationship thing?"

She laughed again, and I felt myself squirm. "*The* relationship. As in the only relationship you've ever had that you were committed to."

"What are you talking about, Maggie?" I couldn't believe she was going to bring up real stuff. We were acting.

"I'm talking about your precious Diane, dear. The only woman you've ever really loved."

"That's not true."

"Yes it is," she said authoritatively. "When she died, you pretty much nixed any chance of any other relationship ever working."

"How?" My voice was suddenly small and I wasn't acting.

"Any time you feel yourself getting close to someone, you pull away. Even better, you continue to choose people who won't love you. Look at that Erica Trinidad. Perfect body, perfect face, and perfect for you. You know why? Because there was no way she was going to love you as much as she loved herself. So she was safe. You just waited until she left you and then you got to start all over."

"I can't believe you're saying this," I said, aghast.

"Of course you can't. But every word is true. Look at that doctor, Allison Crane. The one who was president of that women's organization. Another perfect woman. And totally safe. Why? Because once again, you chose someone who you thought wouldn't love you. But she did, didn't she? So you claimed fidelity to me, and let her go."

"I didn't *claim* fidelity. I felt it."

"Right. And what about me? Why did you choose me?" She stared at me and I tried to swallow. I couldn't believe she was doing this. Everything she said was absolutely true.

"I fell in love with you," I almost whispered.

"But you had no trouble sleeping with another woman while I was gone."

"Maggie! You left me for your ex!"

"Tell me. Was your latest conquest another perfect woman? Or was there something else that made her safe? Where is she now, if you don't mind my asking?"

I thought of Lauren Monroe, now back teaching at Stanford, and knew that Maggie was right. Lauren had been safe, if for no other reason than that I'd always known she'd return to California. It had been a fling at best, anyway. Something to help me get over the pain of Maggie's departure. But I wasn't about to admit that now.

"I do mind," I said. "It's none of your business."

"Good for you!" she said sarcastically. "That's more like it. Get mad!" We were both standing now, glaring at each other. Maggie sat back down. "You see, another therapist would waste all sorts of time on these issues, Cass. In a year or so you might finally realize that what you've been doing is purposely choosing women who couldn't possibly return your love. That way, if they died on you, it wouldn't hurt so bad. That's what it's all about, isn't it? You don't want anyone to get too close, because the pain of losing them would be too much to bear." Her eyes were boring into mine and I knew she wasn't acting at all. I felt my chest constrict.

"Well, it looks like my strategy backfired, then, didn't it?" I said. "I allowed myself to love you, and you left me anyway."

"Yes, I did. And I came back." The silence between us was thick and suffocating. Maggie pointed to the hidden recorder and stood up again. There were tears in her eyes and I realized that this was as difficult for her as it was for me. Somewhere during our charade, things had turned far too real. "If you insist on seeing another therapist, that's your privilege. But you'll never get to the real problem, Cass."

"Which is what?" I dreaded whatever answer she might give. To my relief, she was back in her acting mode.

"That deep down inside, you don't think you deserve to be loved. That's why you pick women who won't love you. That's why you chose me. You like to be beaten, Cass. Just like my other ridiculous clients. Maybe not physically, although I think you'd let me do whatever I wanted to you. But emotionally, you're a pathetic wimp."

"If I'm so pathetic, why do you even bother with me?"

"Isn't it obvious? You need to feel rotten and I need to make you feel rotten. It's how we work, babe.

Don't think I don't understand my own perversities. We're good together, Cass. Opposites attract."

The transition had been so smooth, I wasn't sure where the real stuff left off and the acting began. If it weren't for the tears in her eyes, the compassion on her face, I'd have doubted everything I knew to be true about Maggie Carradine.

"Listen, time's up. I've got a date this morning, but I want you to think about what I've said. I'm sure you'll come to see that I'm right."

"I don't understand. If you like me so weak, why do you want me to be in your therapy group? Why would you want me to get stronger?"

She laughed. "You'll never be stronger. None of them will. They're nothing but a bunch of pitiful losers, every one of them. I want you in the group, Cass, because I enjoy watching you suffer as much as you enjoy suffering. Think about it. I'll see you on Tuesday."

We were both standing again. Maggie held out her hands to me but I pushed past her. She'd had no right to use this phony session to get in all that stuff about Diane, and I was livid. I opened the door, rushed down the hall and practically slammed into Buddy.

"Oh, hi! I didn't know you were here. Are you going to join us?" She was wearing a kayaking outfit that almost matched Maggie's.

"Uh, no. I was just leaving." I tried to act composed but my insides were trembling and my voice sounded funny. "Where are you headed?"

"Grants Pass. There's a level-three run there that should be just right. You sure you don't want to come along?" Her eyes were searching mine, and I wondered if she'd overheard part of what Maggie had said. I was mortified at the thought.

"Uh, no, thanks."

Maggie came out and interceded. "You don't mind closing up, do you, Cass? Buddy and I are running a little late."

"Of course not," I muttered. I watched the two of them leave, inwardly fuming.

Why had she brought up Diane? Did she really believe that I was afraid to commit to another relationship, afraid that someone else would die on me? Was I? I paced the room, my mind racing. I stopped, staring at the yellow mums on the reception desk, and knew she was right. But why had she chosen this venue to enlighten me?

Because you refuse to talk to her, Cassidy, I chided myself. *You never let her close enough to talk about anything real.*

I knew that most of what she'd said was bogus, said only for the sake of whoever was listening in. But interwoven through the b.s. was more truth than I cared to admit.

This wasn't the time to dwell on it, though. Somewhere out there was a killer who'd just heard Maggie's performance, and I needed to figure out who it was. I decided to try Todd Pal again and walked over to Buddy's desk.

She'd left her computer on again, I noticed. Which was great. Maybe Todd Pal had e-mailed me. I quickly logged on and brought up my mail. To my surprise, there was another message from Psychic Junkie and it didn't sound a thing like her:

When all is said and all is done
I hope you know it's not just fun
that makes me do the things I've done.
I'd tell you more but have to run.

I read it over a few times, trying to make sense of the silly rhyme. What had P.J. done? Warned me of danger that didn't exist? Lied to me about telepathic abilities? Had she just strung me along all this time, and now her conscience was getting the best of her? I decided to find out.

"Dear P.J.," I wrote. "What's with the poetry? And what things have you done? Have you been bullshitting me all this time? Once again, I'm Just Curious."

I sent the message and started to lean back in the chair when suddenly Buddy's e-mail chirped. A little box in the upper-right-hand corner flashed, telling her she had new mail. I stared at the flashing box, feeling a trickle of adrenaline in my veins. I leaned forward and slowly composed another message.

"P.J. Tell me this isn't what I think it is." I typed in Psychic Junkie's e-mail address and hit *send*. Once again, Buddy's e-mail box chirped at her. Suddenly, my palms were slick with sweat. I stared at the screen, unbelieving. Buddy was Psychic Junkie? Why? Had she just been playing with me?

I thought back to the first time I'd heard her voice when she'd transferred my call to Maggie. That's when I'd told Maggie of my plan to go on-line in search of a chat group to learn more about psychics. And Maggie's phone had made that weird beeping sound that she attributed to Buddy's problem with transferring calls. Buddy had been listening in! Had she decided then and there to play a trick on Maggie's old girlfriend?

Suddenly, I was furious. What else had Buddy been up to? I wondered. I'd have given anything to get a look at her other mail. Had she pretended to be Claire Voyant, too? And Studly? If only I knew her password.

I tried logging on as *Psychic Junkie* and when the screen asked for my password, I typed in *Buddy*.

Invalid Password. Please try again.

If only I knew her last name. Or something about her. About all I knew was that she liked to kayak. I typed in *kayak* and waited.

Invalid Password. Would you like a hint?

Oh, would I! I loved these programs designed for people who forgot their own passwords. I wondered what kind of hint Buddy had left for herself. I hit the *Yes* box and waited.

What's my favorite letter?

Oh, terrific. That narrows it down, I thought. Most programs only allowed so many invalid tries before shutting down. No way I was going to get twenty-six chances. Suddenly, a thought hit me so unexpectedly that I felt sick to my stomach. Slowly, with trembling fingers, I typed in *BuddyZ*.

The screen flickered and hummed as Buddy's e-mail appeared before me. My heart was pounding.

There they were — every message I'd sent Psychic Junkie as well as those she'd sent me, though none of that really mattered. I had already reached for the phone and was dialing Martha's number, even as my gaze locked onto an unsent outgoing message.

I got Martha's pager and quickly punched in my cell phone number, remembering too late that Martha had turned her pager off in order to avoid talking to Grimes.

"Damn!" I said aloud, slamming down the receiver. My mind reeled when I spotted the heading on the unsent outgoing message. It was addressed to Cassidy James. I clicked the message twice to open it and read the first few lines with a pounding heart.

"Dearest Cassidy. If indeed you're reading this, then my congratulations. You should know that everything on this hard drive is rigged to crash ten minutes after my e-mail is opened, so you don't have much time. And if my e-mail isn't accessed within ten hours of my writing this, the hard drive will self-destruct anyway. Don't you love what you can do with a good virus these days?"

I scrolled down and realized that she'd written a damned novel! There was no way I was going to waste the time reading it. I needed to reach Maggie before they got to Grants Pass.

I yanked open drawers until I found a disk, then inserted it and downloaded Buddy's letter onto the disk. I ejected the disk and ran for the door. I was halfway there when I changed my mind and ran back into the group therapy room, shouting toward the hidden transmitter. "Grimes, if you're listening, Maggie Carradine is in danger. She's on her way to Grants Pass in a silver BMW with two kayaks on the roof-rack. The person with her is probably armed and dangerous. She's already killed at least two people and Maggie may be next on her list. This is not a joke, Grimes. This is for real!" I turned and raced for the front door, not bothering to lock it behind me.

I pushed the Jeep to the limit, half-hoping a cop would pull me over so I could get some assistance. I pulled my thirty-eight from the glove compartment and set it on the seat next to me, putting my foot to the floor. *Think!* I commanded. They had a half-hour's head start. But with the kayaks, they'd be taking it slower than usual. With luck, I might be able to catch them before they got to the river. If only I knew exactly where they were going!

Maybe Buddy had told me, I thought, reaching over with one hand to turn my laptop back on. I waited for it to boot up and then slid Buddy's disk into the slot. It didn't take me long to realize that there was no way I'd be able to read the letter and drive at the same time.

I grabbed my cell phone and prayed that I wasn't already too far out of cell range to make a call. Then I tapped in Todd Pal's number. On the seventh ring, he picked up.

"This better be good," he said. "I've got a hangover and I'm still half-asleep."

"Oh, thank God. Todd, this is Cassidy James."

He cut me off. "Look, I did the best I could. I got your message about two this morning, but I haven't had a chance to even think about it and —"

"That's okay. I need something else. This is really, really important. I figured out who the killer is and I'm on my way to meet her right now. I've got a letter from her but I can't read it and drive at the same time. If I e-mail it to you, can you read it to me over the phone?"

"The killer?"

"It's a long story. This will take a second, hold on." I was now on the windy road that led to Riverland and eventually to Grants Pass. I swerved around a motor home going about two miles an hour and started fumbling with the keys of my laptop, keeping one hand on the wheel.

"Todd, you still there?"

"Yeah, you've got my attention. Should you be talking to the police?"

"I already have," I said. Which wasn't entirely true. I'd paged Martha knowing her pager was turned off, and I'd talked into a transmitting device that I only hoped Grimes was monitoring. "Okay, I'm sending it now."

A moment later, Todd let out a low whistle. "Got it!" he said. "Whoa, this is weird shit."

"Aloud, Todd. Okay?"

I'd gotten behind a logging truck and was looking for a safe place to pass. The road was twisty and I was afraid the cell phone would start to break up soon. Todd read the opening and when he got to the part about the virus, he groaned.

"I hope like hell I didn't just download that virus onto my hard drive! Even with virus protectors you never know."

"Todd, could you hurry, please?"

"Okay, okay. 'Anyway, by now you've probably figured out that it wasn't Harold Bone or Donna Lee who beat Roy to a bloody pulp. And it wasn't sweet Stella Cane who took the bat to Hector Peña. And you know Maylene MacIntyre never would've had the gumption to push her granddad over the cliff. Just like you don't have the gumption to leave the woman who's obviously been abusing you all this time.' " Todd paused, evidently thinking that one over, before he went on. " 'I was so disappointed, Cass. You seem so strong and sure of yourself. To find out that you'd let her treat you like that, well, it makes my blood boil. As you know, I was quite fond of Dr. Carradine. It hurts me to have to do this, but I made a vow. I'm sure you understand. You probably wonder why I'm telling you all this. Why I'd take the chance. It's not much of a chance, though, is it? The odds are with me. For one thing, you'd have to figure out my password. And why would you do that unless you've also figured out that I'm the one who's been sending you and Dr. Carradine your 'dreams'? Of course, I've left you plenty of clues. But still, the odds are on my side.' "

Todd paused and I could hear him draw a deep breath.

"Go on, Todd. Keep reading."

" 'So why am I bothering to write you if I don't think you'll really ever read this? Because, my dear Cassidy, it comforts me to believe that somewhere, there's someone out there who appreciates and understands what I'm doing. I wanted Dr. Carradine to appreciate it, but that didn't work out. I realized that after a while. That's why I started concentrating on you. I wanted you to understand the significance of my work. The hardest part, for me, has been the loneliness. Not being able to tell anyone of my triumphs. Even the greatest moment of my life has been kept secret. You're the only one I've ever been able to share it with. Mother was glorious, you know. Radiant, really. All lit up like a Christmas angel. It was the only time I really loved her, watching her burn to death. Many times, I've wished I'd had the presence of mind to snap a photo of that moment. But never mind. The memory stays with me, as you well know.' "

Todd quit reading and I took the opportunity to pass the logging truck. I didn't know what to say.

"Jesus," he finally muttered. "This is sick. You want me to go on?"

"Yes. And hurry. I'm starting to lose you."

"Okay, okay." He continued in the voice he'd adopted for reading the letter. " 'You never did ask Psychic Junkie the most important question of all, Cass. You should have asked *how* a person becomes this talented at sending! You think I was born with this gift? Well, perhaps, to some extent. But a gift like mine must be developed! Imagine the hours I spent, day after day, year after year, hiding in all the dark places, willing myself not to breathe, stuffed so far down between old blankets or tucked in such tiny crawlspaces that she wouldn't find me. It was in those places, where no light or sound or smell could reach me, that I began to learn to sense where she was. You see, I didn't start out as a sender. In the beginning, I was a true receiver.

" 'I remember vividly the first time I broke through to the other side, so to speak. I was in the trunk and already too big to really fit there. I remember being curled into the fetal position, my nose crammed against my knees, and I sensed her coming. I felt it as clearly as if I could see her. I knew she was looking for me. I knew she had the plastic bat, the one she liked to hit me with as a warmup. My eyes were closed tight and, as I had done many times before, I began to wish fervently that she would go in the other direction. I found myself mentally directing her to turn around and go out into the front yard. I pictured it over and over. *Just turn around*, I told her. It would give me time to scramble out of the trunk and run in the other direction. *Stop right where you are and turn around!* I commanded her. I willed it, much as I had done hundreds of times before. And then something miraculous happened! She did as I directed!

" 'I couldn't actually see her walk outside. I couldn't hear her footsteps, but I knew with every fiber of my being that she had done exactly as I wanted. You've no idea the exhilaration that moment caused! Not just to have escaped discovery. But to have beaten her! To have controlled her! From that moment on, every waking minute of every day, I practiced the fine art of sending.' "

I thought about the innocent child in my dreams and wondered why I hadn't known for sure that she was a girl. Because Buddy hadn't wanted me to, any more than she'd wanted me to know the Bad One was her mother. She was that good at sending, I thought. She wanted me to know how she felt, without giving me enough details to identify her. She had indeed become an expert manipulator. I shivered and forced myself to concentrate on Todd's voice.

" 'She used to look at me so oddly sometimes, shaking her head, like she knew something wasn't right. Not that I could keep her from beating me all the time. But I became a master at misdirection. I sent her false images, buying myself time to get out of her way long enough for one of her "fits" to pass. I don't think she ever really got it until that last day, when she saw me standing at the foot of the stairs, smiling at her. With all my might, I directed her to stay where she was and let herself burn to death.

" 'So, it's time to move on. By the time you learn of the accident, I'll be long gone. And unless you really do read this, you will think it *was* an accident. No reason to suspect otherwise, right? I've done a pretty good job of winning you over, haven't I?

" 'Alas, I realize that you'll probably never lay eyes on these words, but it gives me a little thrill of fear and also excitement to think you might. I will carry that thrill with me, and think of you often. Sweet dreams. Yours truly, Buddy.' " By now, Todd's voice was breaking up badly.

"That's it?" I asked.

"Well, she typed a row of *Z*s across the bottom of the page, but other than that, that's all she wrote." The static between us was growing stronger.

"Todd," I yelled into the phone, "you know what I asked you last night about rearranging the data by fields instead of percentage scores? Do you think you can do that for me? I want all the arson victims whose first and last names start with *Z*." I calculated quickly. If Buddy was really twenty-two like she'd told Maggie, and she was around fifteen when she set her mother's house on fire, then we were looking for something that happened between 1988 and 1992. "That should narrow it down for you," I said.

"I'm having trouble hearing you," he said. "But don't worry. I'll get right on it."

I disconnected, wondering if knowing her real name would make any difference. She no doubt changed her identity at will. If she got away this time, there was no doubt in my mind that she'd start up again somewhere else. The only way to make sure that didn't happen was to catch them before they reached the water and launched their kayaks.

Chapter Sixteen

I tried paging Martha again when I reached Interstate 5 but my cell phone kept flashing the *no service* message, telling me I wasn't close enough to a transmitter to call out. Every time I came around a bend and saw a car up ahead, my heart lurched, thinking I might have caught up to them. But so far, there was no sign of the silver BMW. I kept a nervous eye on my gas gauge, hoping like hell that I'd reach Grants Pass before hitting empty. As it was, it was going to be close.

Finally, the red light that had been warning me for the past five miles refused to go off and I knew I needed to stop. I pulled into a gas station just outside of town and jumped out, waving at the attendant. It's against the law to pump your own gas in Oregon, but I wasn't going to wait around for him to notice me.

"It's an emergency!" I shouted, reaching for the pump. That did the trick. The man came jogging over and practically ripped it out of my hands.

"Can you tell me where they put in around here for whitewater kayaking?"

"Depends," he said, irked at my impatience. "There's half a dozen good spots near here. Depends on what you're looking for."

"They said it was one of the best spots on the Rogue for white water."

"That'd be Moosehead Ridge, probably. Good fishing, too. Wouldn't catch *me* on that stretch of river, though. Starts out tame enough, but from what I hear, it turns nasty right quick."

"Can you tell me how to get there?" I asked, handing him a twenty.

"You don't want me to fill 'er up?"

"No. That'll be fine. Do you know how to get there?"

"Sure. It's not too far from here, in fact. Just go on back to the Interstate and head south for about four miles, then take the Moosehead Junction exit. You'll come to a fork. Take the gravel road that goes off to the right. They put in by the bridge. You can't miss it."

"Keep the change," I said, practically diving into the Jeep. I peeled off, knowing that if it was that close and I hadn't caught up to Maggie and Buddy by now, they may well already be in the water.

Two miles down the road I saw a sign for boat rentals and pulled off, leaping out of the Jeep before I'd even come to a complete stop.

"How much for a kayak?" I asked the startled, bare-chested teenager who was washing down a canoe.

"Thirty bucks an hour. A hundred for the day."

I reached into my wallet and pulled out five twenties, handing them to him. "I'll take this one," I said, heading for a bright red boat that was shorter and wider than the sea kayak I was used to. "Can you give me a hand?"

"Hey, you gotta fill out forms and stuff. You can't just take one. I need to make a copy of your driver's license and stuff like that."

I took out two more twenties. "Come on, this is an emergency. You can keep my PowerBook as collateral."

"As what?"

"Think of it as a deposit. You can keep it till I bring the boat back. Okay?" I bent over to pick up the kayak and was surprised it wasn't heavier. About thirty pounds, I figured. It was more awkward than heavy.

The kid looked around, shrugged and helped me slide the kayak into the back of the Jeep. "You got your own PFD?" he said, handing me a double-bladed paddle.

I looked at him blankly.

"Personal floatation device." He rolled his eyes. "Life vest. Here. Take this. You need a helmet, too, and your spray-skirt. I shouldn't be doing this without getting your information."

"Here," I said. I took out my driver's license and handed it to him. "I'll be back. Honest."

"Okay. But just in case, where you headed? It's one of the questions we're supposed to ask.

"Just up the road," I said. "Moosehead Ridge."

"Great choice!" he said enthusiastically. "You sure you can handle class three?"

"No sweat," I said, lying. "I do it all the time." I smiled reassuringly and pulled back onto the highway, hoping that the boat would be an unnecessary precaution.

I found Moosehead Junction and followed the gas station attendant's directions, feeling a growing sense of dread with each mile that I didn't see Maggie's car. What if they'd gone somewhere else? Buddy had said they were going to the best whitewater spot, though. And everyone seemed to agree that Moosehead Ridge was it. But maybe with Maggie's limited experience, they'd chosen a tamer route. Which would make sense, I thought, if they were just out for a day of fun. But for what Buddy had in mind, I suspected Moosehead Ridge would be her natural choice.

The gravel road gave way to dirt just as I reached the bridge. A clearing, large enough for half a dozen cars, had been carved out of the hillside, and Maggie's silver BMW glinted in the sunlight. My pulse raced as I scanned the area for them. There was only one other vehicle in sight, a yellow Corvette parked near the water's edge. I spotted a couple necking inside and ran to their door, banging on it.

"Hey!" the kid inside shouted, startled.

"Did you see the people in that car get into the

water?" I asked, searching the river for a sign of them. The water appeared fairly calm, I thought.

"Yeah. They left about ten minutes ago."

"Damn!" I said. "How far does this road go?" I pointed to the winding single-lane dirt path that led downstream.

"Just to the bottom of Little Moose. It's the turn-around point for the class three stretch. Most people stop there and have someone drive them back up here. Otherwise, they have to run the Ridge and that's way rougher water. Classic class five."

"You think I can catch them before they get to the Ridge if I take the road?"

"No way. The road takes forever. It's twice as fast by boat."

"Damn!

"Come on, I'll help you launch." He climbed out of the Corvette and uncoiled a six-foot frame that housed nothing but bunched muscles and sinew. He lumbered over to my Jeep and pulled the boat out by himself, lofting it over his shoulder as if it were made of balsa wood. "Get your gear," he said.

I followed him down the dirt path to the river, noting the posted signs that warned of rough water ahead, and put on my helmet and PFD while he set the little boat in the water.

My heart started to skip. "So how exactly do I know when this first stretch quits being class three and changes to class five?" I asked, fastening the spray-skirt around my waist.

The kid laughed. "Oh, you'll hear it before you see it. Just stay to the right when you get to where the river forks and you'll drift right over to the bank, no problem. You can't miss it. There's a sandy beach where everyone pulls out and a parking lot sorta like this one. You do know what you're doing?" he asked, holding the boat steady while I struggled into it.

"More or less." I wiggled my body down into the cockpit and took a deep breath, adjusting my weight for balance. Without my even asking, the kid helped me attach the spray-skirt to the cockpit rim.

He furrowed his brow. "It's usually best to go with another boat, in case you run into trouble. If you wait a while, someone else will probably come along. This place will be hopping pretty soon."

"Thanks," I said. "I don't suppose you'd like to serve as my guide?" I tried to make it sound like I was kidding.

"Uh, we didn't bring our boats today," he said, looking sheepishly back toward the Corvette.

I ignored the lump of fear that rose in my throat, and used my paddle to push myself away from the bank. For better or worse, I was on my way. I cleared my mind of the rising panic and concentrated on the fact that I needed to catch up to Maggie before Buddy managed to stage their accident.

The river was wide but the current was stronger than it had looked from shore. I practiced some basic paddle strokes and the kayak moved gracefully through the water with relative ease. It was a good time to try a few leans, I thought. Forcing my body to relax, I shifted my weight to first one side and then the other, feeling the pressure change against my knees as I put the boat on edge. The little boat danced over a ripple, causing a flurry in the pit of my stomach. I passed a small boulder to my left and practiced turning into the eddy, toward the calm water just behind the boulder. I positioned the boat slightly sideways from the eddy, paused for a second, gauging the speed I'd need, then took three deep pulls on the paddle and surged forward. It looked for a moment as if I would hit the boulder, but at the last second, the current carried me deep into the eddy and I tilted up on edge to keep myself right-side-up.

I allowed myself a brief moment of exhilaration while I rested, scanning the river downstream for potential hazards. Then, knowing I didn't have the luxury of taking any more time, I paddled away from the safety of the eddy and into the gathering current.

It didn't take long for the tiny ripples to become small waves. The kayak glided over them easily, however, and all I had to do was keep the bow pointed forward while I kept my balance. I used the paddles for direction more than speed as I maneuvered past the few obstacles I encountered. I was beginning to feel confident in my skills, when the river made a bend and suddenly the little waves became larger.

The current had also become more powerful and now things were rushing past me. I studied the river ahead, trying to anticipate my next move. Most of the boulders were large and round, but here and there a tree snag jutted out from the bank and I steered around them, trying to keep in the center of the main channel. I rounded another bend and suddenly found myself heading sideways toward a boulder.

"Think!" I shouted. My natural inclination was to lean away from it, but I knew that wasn't right. There would be a natural pillow of water buffeting off the rock, which should protect me. By leaning the wrong way, I'd most likely end up overturned. Against my inner warnings, I leaned my body and boat aggressively toward the rock, even putting my hand out against it. To my relief, the boat glanced off the boulder and headed back downstream as if nothing had happened. But my heart was in my throat.

There was little time to relish my triumph over the rock, however. Once I'd rounded the last bend, the river had narrowed and at the same time become more treacherous. If this was only class three, I never wanted to see anything higher!

Boulders now lined both sides of the river, creating a narrow passageway. There was no mistaking what was meant by the word *whitewater*, I thought. The waves frothed and churned as they carried me over them, past the protection of eddies I had no hope of reaching, past the safety of the shoreline I couldn't reach if I wanted to.

Which I did, I told myself. I'd have given almost anything to be sitting on the safety of dry land.

Snap out of it! I chided myself. There was no time for cowardice. I needed to reach the base of Little Moose before Buddy had a chance to carry out her plan.

Jeez! I thought. If this was Little Moose, I hated to think what Big Moose was like.

There you go again, thinking like a coward.

I shook my head, trying to concentrate on the raging water in front of me, and suddenly, a terrifying thought struck me. Could Buddy be sending me these conflicting thoughts? Did she somehow know I was coming? Was she trying to psych me out?

I thought of her standing at the base of the stairs, willing her mother to stand still while she burned to death, and a shiver ran right through me. Suddenly, out of nowhere, a boulder rose up in front of me and before I could maneuver around it, before I could even think what to do, I slammed into it. The kayak went up on edge and rolled over. Suddenly, I was upside down in the water.

Think! I commanded. *You've got to flip the boat back over!* I rocked my torso, feverishly trying to right the boat. *Calm down! Use your hips. Right the boat and let your torso follow.* It was as if the words in my head were being shouted by an impatient instructor. Quelling the rising panic, I closed my eyes, snapped my hip upward and rotated my body as the kayak rolled right-side-up. I gasped for air, holding my heaving sides, even as the boat surged forward. I'd done it! My heart pounded and water streamed down my face, but I was still alive. More determined than ever, I scanned the river ahead of me, searching for the fork that would lead me to safety, and hopefully to Maggie.

The kid back at the parking lot was right. I heard it long before I saw it. Just like that, the sound of rushing water gave way to a mild roar that made my neck hairs stand at attention. I immediately veered toward the right, even before the river wanted me to. When I saw the river divide, I nearly shouted with joy. There was a clear delineation between the right side and the left. It was as if half of the river had decided to call it quits, while the other half said, *the hell with you, I'm going on!*

I angled the boat toward the sandy beach, my eyes scouring the shoreline for Buddy and Maggie. Their boats were not on shore. Had they already dragged them up onto the bank? I paddled up to the sandy spit and studied the bank. There were no footprints, no drag marks in the sand. Last night's tide had covered any previous markings. No one had stopped here yet today.

"Damn it!" I shouted at the top of my lungs. My voice was lost in the distant roar of the river. Now what was I supposed to do?

"You're not afraid of getting wet, are you?" Buddy had teased me once. It was almost if she were taunting me with the same words now. Daring me to chase after her, daring me to do something I shouldn't even consider.

"Shit!" I shouted again, pushing myself away from the safety of the sheltered beach. Before I could talk myself out of it, using long deep strokes I paddled myself out to the source of the roar, to the left side of the river, toward Big Moose.

The river wanted me, I thought, surprised at how the current pulled me right into its channel, sucking me downstream like a vacuum. I tried to relax, knowing a stiff torso would be harder to balance, but my heart was pounding. I used the paddles to brace the kayak, keeping it steady in the roiling water. Suddenly, the bottom dropped out of the river and I was headed nose-down into a steep drop. I leaned back, willing the bow to rise, bracing myself against the impact. Despite my efforts, the bow knifed into the water and the boat turned sideways, banging against a boulder. Before I could even lean into the rock, the boat bounced off, caroming off another rock as if I was in a pinball machine. Somehow, through sheer luck, I managed to remain upright.

Desperately, I worked the paddles, trying to coerce the bow forward. Just as I did, the river dropped again, but this time I was able to throw my weight toward the stern in time and the kayak handled the four-foot fall with relative ease, landing in somewhat calmer water.

And then I saw them! Both kayaks were resting in an eddy not two hundred feet away. My heart hammered as I surveyed the situation. Maggie looked fine. At least from where I was, they appeared to be having a good time.

I shot forward, my mind racing. Should I confront Buddy here in the river? Or pretend not to know what was happening? Before I could decide, she spotted me. I maneuvered the kayak across the stream to the eddy line and turned into the calmer water, nearly capsizing when I put the boat on edge.

Buddy laughed. "Not bad for someone who claims to be the still-water type!" she shouted over the roar.

"What in the world are you doing here, Cass?" Maggie was soaking wet and looked shaken.

"Decided to join you!" I shouted. "How come you guys didn't stop back there where the river divided?"

"Why should we?" Maggie asked, raising her voice against the roar of the water.

"Because that was the end of the class three section. You're in class five now!"

Maggie looked from me to Buddy, obviously puzzled.

"Really?" Buddy said, looking surprised. "No wonder it picked up! I thought it was kinda rough." Her dark eyes were studying me, and a small smile played on her lips.

I looked pointedly at Maggie. "I think we should get out *here*, Maggie. If we can get over to that bank we can walk back up to the divide. It's not that far."

"You go ahead, if you want," Buddy shouted.

"Maggie's doing just fine. I told you she was a natural!"

Maggie was looking from Buddy to me, her green eyes probing.

"I really think we should get out here," I repeated, my eyes pleading with her.

"Actually, I *am* pretty tired. You don't mind, do you, Buddy? This was a lot more strenuous than I thought."

Buddy's eyes narrowed. She was holding onto one end of Maggie's paddle, keeping the two boats steady. She started shaking her head. "You did it, didn't you?" she said, looking at me. Her voice had lowered and it was difficult to hear her over the water rushing past us.

"You made it too easy," I said. "You wanted me to know."

"Know what?" Maggie asked.

"Who I really am," Buddy said. "I didn't think you'd actually do it. This kind of changes things."

"Do what?" Maggie's voice had risen.

"Figure out her password, for one thing. Read the letter she wrote before her hard drive crashed. Realize that she's the one who's been sending us our dreams. She's a murderer, Maggie."

Maggie had started to pull away from Buddy's boat, but Buddy had a firm grip on the paddle and wouldn't let go.

"It sounds terrible when you put it that way," Buddy said. "*Murderer* has such a nasty ring to it."

"What would you like me to call you?" I said, struggling to keep my boat in the eddy. My stern kept trying to drag me downstream, but I couldn't move any closer without getting within Buddy's reach.

"I never hurt anyone who didn't have it coming," she said. "You of all people should understand that. I'm just doing what you do, Cass. Fighting the bad guys. I'm just better at it than you. I make sure they never hurt anyone else again."

Maggie looked incredulous. "But someone hit you on the head and stole the file!" she said.

Buddy laughed and pantomimed hitting herself over the head.

"The problem with playing judge and jury," I said, "is what if you're wrong?"

"I haven't been wrong yet," she said, flashing her Donnie Osmond smile.

"You're wrong about Maggie."

"Bullshit! I heard you in there groveling! You let her hit you! She's no better than the assholes who abuse her clients. In fact, she's worse. She's a liar and a hypocrite. She deserves to be punished."

"Oh, God," Maggie said, shaking her head, still trying to pull free from Buddy's boat. "Buddy, that was a trap. We found the transmitter and made that whole scene up —"

Buddy cut her off, though she looked momentarily unsure. "It wasn't just then, Maggie. I've seen the way Cassidy looks at you. I've heard her on the phone. You hurt her. You weren't just making it up. I'd know! You're just trying to save yourself!"

"She's telling the truth, Buddy. We were trying to lay a trap!"

"You think I'm going to believe you? You're just like all the other victims, trying to protect their abusers! God, I can't believe I thought you were different. The pair of you are sickening!"

"I would never hurt Cassidy, Buddy. I love her."

"Oh sure. That's why you left her for someone else!"

"That wasn't something I wanted to do. It was something I had to do. There's a difference."

"And you just expected her to wait around for you?"

"I didn't expect her to. I hoped she would. I wanted her to. But I didn't expect it of her." Maggie was looking at me now and I saw tears in her eyes.

Buddy was shaking her head, looking from Maggie to me. "You don't buy this, do you?"

"Yeah, I do, Buddy. There's no reason for you to hurt Maggie. She's never hurt anyone in her life."

"Bullshit! You forget I'm not just a sender. You don't think I've been able to read how you feel? And now you're saying she didn't hurt you?"

"My feelings were hurt, Buddy, but that's part of life. I've accepted what Maggie did, what she had to do. It wasn't easy for me, but I'm over it. It was between Maggie and me, and it's over." Saying it aloud, I realized it was true. And suddenly I felt stronger than I'd felt in ages.

Maggie tried once again to pull her paddle free from Buddy's grip and this time, Buddy let go unexpectedly, causing Maggie's boat to spin backward. Buddy leaned forward and yanked the paddle away, then used it to shove Maggie out into the swirling current.

"No!" I yelled.

"You want her so bad, you can have her," Buddy said. "But you gotta catch her first." With that, she wheeled around and expertly dug into the water, moving away from the eddy in sure, even strokes.

Much more awkwardly than she had done, I

pointed my bow downstream and took off after them. I saw Maggie's kayak rounding the bend, skidding along on its side. Buddy was right behind her.

I let the current guide me, using my paddles not just for balance now, but for power. The river plunged several feet and this time I rode it out, leaning back, never missing a beat with the paddles. A boulder loomed up on my right and I leaned into it, letting the pocket of water around it cushion the blow. They were no more than thirty feet in front of me, but it seemed an impossible distance. Maggie's kayak was caroming off of rocks, swirling around in the water like a bobber. Buddy was almost on top of her. Suddenly, I found myself willing her to stop.

Let her go, Buddy! Let her go and we'll let you go. Don't hurt her, please!

To my surprise, Buddy turned around and our eyes made contact. Even from that distance, I could see her dark eyes dancing.

Deal! she seemed to say, though even if she'd shouted it, I wouldn't have heard her over the roar. She pulled up next to Maggie's kayak and, leaning her own boat dangerously, flipped Maggie's over. Then she looked back at me once more before shooting down the rapids in front of her.

"Roll over!" I yelled, though I knew Maggie couldn't hear me under the water. I'd almost reached her when her boat snagged itself on a tangle of tree branches jutting out from the bank. Maggie was trapped underwater. "Goddamn you!" I yelled after Buddy, who was long gone.

My boat was swirling away from the tree branch, caught in the larger current, and in a second, I'd be past Maggie's kayak. I had no choice. I leaned all the way over and turned my own kayak upside down, holding my breath as I tried to orient myself underwater. I grabbed hold of the skirt release and pulled it away from me, then off of the cockpit. Damn it! I could feel myself being swept downstream, away from Maggie.

I pushed myself out of the boat, struggling to work my legs free. Suddenly, the boat bounced away and I popped to the surface, gulping the fresh air. I looked around frantically and saw Maggie's kayak scoot past me, on a path that followed my own. But where was Maggie? Already swept downstream? Or still trapped underwater?

"Maggie!" I yelled. I was being swept downstream and couldn't fight the current. *Float on your back feet-first*, I heard Buddy's voice say. If only I'd taken notes on that film! The PFD kept my body and head above water as I strained to see over the white rapids, searching for any sign of Maggie, for any chance to rest. The river rushed around a bend and suddenly I saw her. She was draped across a tree snag right in front of me. If I plowed into her, she might lose the tenuous grip she had and be dragged back into the water. But if I didn't try to grab the branch, I might not get another chance.

"Hold on!" I yelled. I flipped over onto my stomach and, using every ounce of strength in my body, pulled myself through the water toward the branch. A second later, my arms were draped over the branch, even while the river tugged at my legs.

"Thank God," Maggie yelled. Even though she was right beside me, the noise was deafening. "I thought you'd drowned!"

"Can you pull yourself up?" I asked, feeling my arms tremble against the weight.

"I'm trying!"

"Just inch yourself over, like on the monkey bars!" I yelled. "That's it! I'm right behind you!"

Slowly, hand over hand, Maggie and I worked our way sideways toward the bank of the river. By the time we reached safety, we both collapsed in the mud.

An eternity passed before our breathing became less ragged and we were able to sit up. Suddenly, Maggie reached over and grabbed my arm. "Did you hear that?" We were both trembling, more from exhaustion than the cold, I guessed, though if we didn't get out of our wet clothes soon, we might need to worry about hypothermia.

"Hear what?" I asked, straining to hear past the roar of the river.

"That," she said, looking at me oddly, cocking her head.

"Yeah. I think I *did* hear it." I got to my feet and Maggie stood up beside me on wobbly legs.

"It sounded like someone laughing," she said.

I felt my pulse quicken. "That's funny. To me it sounded like a little girl crying."

We looked at each other and a shared shiver ran through us. It occurred to us both that Buddy had just sent us her own peculiar good-bye.

"Cass, about what I said back there. About Diane. I shouldn't have done that. I was out of line and —"

"Maggie. Be quiet. You're smart and you're beautiful and I love you, but sometimes you talk too damn much." I pulled her to me and covered her lips with mine.

Epilogue

It was Sergeant Grimes, of all people, who found us. I never thought I'd be happy to see the s.o.b., but I suppose the same could be said for him. We actually hugged, before common sense kicked in and we remembered we hated each other.

Maggie and I gave our depositions, doing our best to keep Martha out of it. There was no point in jeopardizing her career. Harold Bone was let go and an all-points bulletin was put out for Buddy. That was before they found her kayak downstream, battered and broken, lodged in an outcropping where it had come to its final rest.

Though they searched the river for days, using dogs and dragging the bottom where they could, her body was never found. She was unofficially thought dead, but her case would stay open until her remains were found.

Maggie had been afraid of how the group members might handle what Buddy had done, but surprisingly, it had brought them closer together and the group was going strong. We decided not to mention my role in the whole thing and I simply dropped out of the group.

"I still don't get the Z thing," Grimes said to me during our last discussion on the matter. We were in his office, Maggie on one side of me, Martha on the other, though she was keeping pretty quiet. Grimes had gone over the conversations he'd recorded until he was blue in the face, though he knew he could never use them in court, if it ever came to that.

I thought of my last e-mail from Todd Pal. He'd finally found the link we'd wanted: a suspected child-beater who'd died in a house fire. She hadn't shown up in the initial search of rural areas, but when he expanded the search to include cities, he'd found Thelma Moore right smack dab in the middle of Austin, Texas. I thought of the slightly Southern lilt in Buddy's speech and felt sure he'd found Buddy's mother.

Todd, who'd become consumed with curiosity over the case, went above and beyond the call of duty, and his summary was enlightening. According to the local sheriff's records, no one knew whatever happened to the woman's daughter. At first they thought she'd died in the fire, but her remains were never found. Since no one had seen the kid in years, including neighbors and school officials, there was speculation, based on early child-abuse reports, that the mother might have killed her and buried her somewhere on the property. They'd brought in dogs, hoping to unearth a child's grave, but the effort proved fruitless and they abandoned this theory. One neighbor said she thought the girl had gone to live with a relative, but an exhaustive search revealed no next of kin on record.

The fire and subsequent burning death of Thelma Moore was finally ruled a suicide and the case was closed. Buddy, the forgotten child, had gotten away with the perfect murder.

I hadn't shared this information with anyone else and I wasn't sure why. Maybe if Grimes had Buddy's real name, he could trace her somehow. *If* she was still alive. It might save the lives of others down the road. The lives of other abusers.

"You think maybe her last name's got a *Z* in it?" Grimes was asking.

"I guess we'll never know," I said. "I think she fancied herself a modern-day Zorro. Out there righting wrongs, giving the bad guys a taste of their own medicine."

"Hmph," Grimes mumbled. "It just don't make any sense."

But in a way, it did.

Maggie shot me a knowing look and Martha, glancing up, caught it. I smiled innocently at Martha and reached over to squeeze Maggie's hand.

"Not in here, you don't. Get on out of here, all

three of you. Cripes. This whole damn town's run through with lesbos."

We left, laughing, and walked out into the afternoon sunshine.

"Tina says if you come over for dinner tonight, she'll cook Italian." Martha's eyes were dancing. "Unless you two have other plans."

"Maybe a rain check?" Maggie said. There was no mistaking the husky tone of her voice, and I didn't have to be psychic to know what she had in mind.

A few of the publications of
THE NAIAD PRESS, INC.
P.O. Box 10543   Tallahassee, Florida 32302
Phone (850) 539-5965
Toll-Free Order Number: 1-800-533-1973
Web Site: WWW.NAIADPRESS.COM
Mail orders welcome. Please include 15% postage.
Write or call for our free catalog which also features an
incredible selection of lesbian videos.

SIXTH SENSE by Kate Calloway. 224 pp. 6th Cassidy James
mystery.   ISBN 1-56280-228-3 $11.95

DAWN OF THE DANCE by Marianne K. Martin. 224 pp. A dance
with an old friend, nothing more . . . yeah!   ISBN 1-56280-229-1   11.95

WEDDING BELL BLUES by Julia Watts. 240 pp. Love, family,
and a recipe for success.   ISBN 1-56280-230-5   11.95

THOSE WHO WAIT by Peggy J. Herring. 160 pp. Two
sisters . . . in love with the same woman.   ISBN 1-56280-223-2   11.95

WHISPERS IN THE WIND by Frankie J. Jones. 192 pp. "If you
don't want this," she whispered, "all you have to say is 'stop.' "
                                                       ISBN 1-56280-226-7   11.95

WHEN SOME BODY DISAPPEARS by Therese Szymanski.
192 pp. 3rd Brett Higgins mystery.   ISBN 1-56280-227-5   11.95

THE WAY LIFE SHOULD BE by Diana Braund. 240 pp. Which
one will teach her the true meaning of love?   ISBN 1-56280-221-6   11.95

UNTIL THE END by Kaye Davis. 256pp. 3rd Maris Middleton
mystery.   ISBN 1-56280-222-4   11.95

FIFTH WHEEL by Kate Calloway. 224 pp. 5th Cassidy James
mystery.   ISBN 1-56280-218-6   11.95

JUST YESTERDAY by Linda Hill. 176 pp. Reliving all the
passion of yesterday.   ISBN 1-56280-219-4   11.95

These are just a few of the many Naiad Press titles — we are the oldest and
largest lesbian/feminist publishing company in the world. We also offer an
enormous selection of lesbian video products. Please request a complete
catalog. We offer personal service; we encourage and welcome direct mail
orders from individuals who have limited access to bookstores carrying our
publications.